Sacred Remembrances

Sacred Remembrances

A Collection of Chronicles by Saint Peter the Apostle
Translated from the Greek by Alistair Chapman
and Fellows of Jesus Emmanuel College

PETER ROBERTS

RESOURCE *Publications* · Eugene, Oregon

SACRED REMEMBRANCES

A Collection of Chronicles by Saint Peter the Apostle Translated from the Greek by Alistair Chapman and Fellows of Jesus Emmanuel College

Resource Publications
An Imprint of Wipf and Stock Publishers
199 W. 8th Ave., Suite 3
Eugene, OR 97401

www.wipfandstock.com

PAPERBACK ISBN: 979-8-3852-5751-5
HARDCOVER ISBN: 979-8-3852-5752-2
EBOOK ISBN: 979-8-3852-5753-9
VERSION NUMBER 12/05/25

For Bronwen, Alison, Prudence, and Thomas

CONTENTS

Preface

Dear Reader,

This novel is obviously a work of historical fiction.

No such chronicles by Saint Peter have ever been found or (probably) were ever written, and as far as I know, there is no such school as the Jesus Emmanuel College.

The work is based on the Gospels and the Acts and the letters of Saint Paul and Saint Peter with supplementary sources.

Biblical passages such as in the sayings of Jesus have been, in the main, paraphrased and/or altered to suit the fictional, pre-Gospel narrative, for historical authenticity.

I have noted biblical references where direct translations (in *italics*) have been made in the copyright section.

PR

Foreword by the Translator

THE DISCOVERY OF THE TEXTS in 1990 carrying the name of Saint Peter was a revelation of unimaginable proportions. For many years scholars and archeologists pored over the texts in high expectation and finally announced they were genuine five years later. The parchments were in good order and most of the script was legible.

I, as leader of the Jesus Emmanuel College at the time, along with a team from the college, was asked to translate the texts from Koine Greek. We did this with assiduity to present what you have before you today.

The discovery of the texts was the work of a team of amateur archeologists who came across the catacomb where, just like the Dead Sea Scrolls, they had remained buried for millennia. I won't bore you with the details of their uncovering but suffice to say the texts were the most exciting discovery since the Scrolls. The writings are not by Peter himself, as he explains, but by a copier or scribe who wrote down what he was told.

We do not know for sure whether the chronicles were written in one sitting or present a continual account of happenings and sayings on the circuit. We suspect that the original was in Arabic, and the Greek was a later translation, perhaps by the scribe himself. Most of the writings confirm what's written in the later Gospels, but there are fascinating and important insights from Peter about Jesus, his women followers, the apostles, Paul, and the early church that have antagonized theologians and scholars for centuries.

Some sections are more revelatory than others but the overall impression of Peter as man and saint combine to instill a renewed life and vigor into the Gospels.

We do not know who the scribe was, but guesses have been made including John Mark, Matthew, or James the Just, or even John the Evangelist.

Not that it matters. The writer has actually included a foreword which is also revealing.

I leave these words at your disposal, dear reader, whether Christian or atheist, as the man Cephas, Simon Peter, stands vulnerable yet dignified and all too human before us, and his Lord.

AC

Introduction by the Scribe

I write as one of the many who followed Jesus. Of the many, Simon Peter was the first, and although not my closest companion, he approached me, his brother, in Jerusalem, to write for him this history.

I remain anonymous as anonymity brings with it a universal voice. I did not rewrite anything of what Peter told me. I simply searched for words with more accuracy and fluency, occasionally, after asking for clarity.

Firstly, I tell you about my relationship with Peter and how I traveled with him as a fellow disciple willing to illuminate, however briefly, the man and his presence through his personal contact with Jesus. I was not the closest to Peter, but was always near him, and he took me under his wing, and at times we shared some discussion and thoughts, but in the main, we were separate and non-conversant. So, I was astounded when he chose me to write these chronicles.

Everything is as Peter told to me, and nothing shall be added to or deleted by those who succeed him.

I want to be certain from the beginning that I had no intention of recording anything our Lord Jesus said or did from my own recollections. We lay in the flower bed of his words as in a dream, or on a cloud. Words are heavy and drag us down from our meditation to express that which is never meant to be burdened with a scripture.

Yet, Peter convinced me that our discipleship should be presented to our followers so that all may partake in its experience, to better understand Jesus and his ministry. We who shared his life know too well his true character. Peter's writings are not to convince anyone of anything, but to give substance and credence to the Messiah who walked the earth in the hope of redeeming humanity through the law of love and personal sacrifice.

Such a man is great, and his greatness will live on throughout history, for never such a law has been acted, never such a man seen, never such a life lived or death experienced.

Peter shared closely with Jesus his thoughts and intentions and prayers, closer than any of his brothers, so the two were like one, and I humbly accepted the offer of relating Peter's discourses because I was taught to write in Hebrew and Greek, and I so respected Peter that I could not deny him.

Much of what I write I cannot vouch for, and simply relate the events and dialogues as told to me. Peter often conferred with the apostles to recount Jesus' words which I know ensued in some debate, and during his lifetime an oral tradition developed which Peter also utilized.

The discourses of Jesus and Peter and the apostles are an intimate rendering of Peter the man that you might know him better.

Anon

I

From Bethsaida to Capernaum

I, Simon Peter, Cephas, will tell of my time with the Lord, before and after his death, and relate what passed between us and his disciples, what I heard and saw, and how we lived together as humble servants and friends.

I was born in Bethsaida and when I was of age, I married, and my wife fell quickly with child, but it was not to be. Both mother and child died during birth. I then left my mother and my father, Jonah, while my younger brother Andrew stayed with them until he finished his religious instruction, and I moved to Capernaum where I worked as a fisherman on the Sea of Galilee, taught by Zebedee, and was welcomed by him and his wife Salome, and sons John and James, to their community.

Jonah and his sons were known to my family. They were friends in Bethsaida before they moved to Capernaum. However, after the death of my wife, my mother-in-law, Rachael, asked to come with me since she was for two years widowed, and then childless, and so she accompanied me to Capernaum.

We lived for a little while in the house of Zebedee since it had many rooms and two floors and they were pleased to help us. Their house had a large courtyard where animals wandered and people worked. With their help I built a small house not far from their place on their land near a separate row of houses that he owned, so I could extend the house in time.

It was a simple stone hut with a flattened earthen floor and a roof made of straw mats thrown over a few wooden trusses, but with strong foundations, as Zebedee instructed. There were only two rooms at first but it afforded shelter, with a small bath and a straw bed in each room. But my mother-in-law remained in Zebedee's house at night and spent the day in my house cleaning and cooking until it could be extended.

A little later Andrew, after he had been instructed in the law, joined us at Capernaum while my other siblings remained in Bethsaida. I started a small vegetable garden in the front, and Zebedee's wife helped plant the first vegetables of beans, and lentils, and onions. I did not keep animals as Zebedee did, for he was regarded as wealthy, and his sons were good fisherman and he also brought food to our table when needed. He also traded in the village market and had contracts to supply fish to Jerusalem.

When we spoke, our discourse was simple and I was instructed in some of the Mosaic laws, especially purification and ritual. At first, I had no boat but rented one from Zebedee and worked with his sons under their instructions.

The fish I caught I ate or sold, and the living was meek but sufficient, and so we lived from day to day. We took bread from Zebedee's house, and a little meat when we could afford it.

Andrew's help with fishing was much appreciated and he worked hard and we sometimes managed to catch more than our needs. Zebedee bought our surplus and my mother-in-law tended the garden, helped mend the nets and sails, and she was always bright and amiable, and we soon extended the house by adding another room so we could all live together.

Andrew was also a dreamer. It was hard to reach him at times but he worked well and was always agreeable. Gradually, however, he wandered for days from the house. When he returned, he told us of a man, a baptizer, whom he had chance to see, and he cleansed men and women in the River Jordan in Judea near Jericho. He said he was called John and he spoke of the imminent coming of the Messiah, and acted humbly and lived simply like an animal in the wilderness.

I had heard of such men in the Greek world who were called beasts because they willingly lived on the streets eating scraps and living without shelter or clothes, and not caring less about anything.

But then John was one of us, a Jewish prophet, according to Andrew. I knew little of Elijah but it was said that John was Elijah reborn, and John spoke of the things Elijah had prophesized, and he, John, announced that a new man, a leader, was born to renew the world, and his time had arrived.

I let these things pass because I was tired and occupied, and sometimes we had but a few fish and little to eat. The work was hard, the nets heavy, and they were often torn and damaged and needed repairing, and some days the waters were high when the wind tore across the sea, and we huddled in our houses and waited for the calm. We attended our callouses and blistered, water-dried, sunburnt hardened hands with a natural balm provided by Zebedee's sons. But some days the agony in our hands and arms and shoulders was unbearable, and we could not work.

But the talk about John increased and it was said by Zebedee that he had drawn the attention of Sadducees and the Roman authorities. And in the marketplace people spoke of him admiringly as perhaps the Messiah himself and the leader they were wanting. We knew of a community which lived an exemplary life in the wilderness, and it was said John was one of them originally but now preached and lived alone.

This isolated community upheld the Scriptures and exemplified the life of the truly pious. They were called Essenes, and they lived around Judea and at Qumran on what nature provided, which was scant, and dressed roughly and never married, and they immersed themselves in water every day as a ritual, and when I asked more about them I was told they were the new community of God, come to show the wayward Jews how they had wandered from the righteous path of the Scriptures, and why God would bring punishment upon them.

It was said John was taught by the Essenes, and one day I went with Andrew, as he insisted, to a gathering where John was preaching at a place called Aenon, not far from Capernaum. Andrew was a follower, and I was worried he might become one of them, an adherent or devotee, and leave home. He was infatuated, but I was wary of these prophets and distrusted most men who said they were sent by God, yet not announced by God, but this one was said to be anointed.

The man stood on a large craggy rock on the shore and many gathered close to hear him. He was small in size and had long unkempt hair and a dark beard and looked overall lamentable, but not old. He was not gray. He wore a coarse covering said to be of camel hair and a large twisted leather belt. He spoke with a strong voice but still his words were passed down to those who stood at the back who could not hear. And there were whispers when he spoke but, mainly, the crowd was quiet and listened to his words, which were few but solemn.

People were impressed; they had never seen a baptism before but the significance of ritual cleansing was already understood by us. He repeated the word "repent" again and again, and that "salvation" was at hand. Was John the liberator? What did he mean by "repent?" Did we not make sacrifices? Keep the commandments? Go about our work honestly? And what was this "salvation?" Freedom from the Romans?

People thus questioned and discussed. John was forthright in reply and his message was clear and echoed what I had heard about him. He said the day of the Lord is at hand, it is now, and to prepare, for he has sent one before him who would be the supreme sacrifice.

Then they asked how they should prepare? So, they brought John ritual offerings, as they had been taught. He sneered at them and said something like, "Now you come for security with your offerings, but unless you turn your heart, none shall be saved. For the Lord demands justice and mercy, not animals and oil."

He then baptized men and women in the water as they came to him by the river by holding their backs and fully immersing them in the clear water, and they became his disciples. They said they would go forth and pay taxes that they owed, and sell fairly, and pay fully for what they bought, and sell what they did not need and give to those with less, as they were instructed, in preparation and repentance. Others went back to their old ways ignoring the warning.

We left the scene and the people dispersed back to their villages and John sat on his rock staring out to sea as the sun set. He looked content, and was even smiling, with one leg raised, sitting on the other, and most of the people talked together of his words and the unorthodox process of cleansing which became known locally as baptism, and John became John the baptizer—or simply, the baptist.

Andrew asked me what I thought of him. I said he was surely devout and knew things we did not know, but that didn't mean he was from God.

I had heard that there were many preachers about this time and they did amazing things. They could cure the sick and make the blind see and they declared themselves prophets, but some were put to death by the Pharisees as being false and blasphemous, but still they came, and some had large followings as they proclaimed a new dawn for the people of Israel.

And the Roman authorities also watched them warily for any signs of insurrection—if they preached a message of defiance they could be arrested, or of protest, or if their following became too great—and many did provoke retribution in their zeal, and were arrested and executed as zealots or rebels by the Romans. So, the stories spread of these preachers and miracle workers and false messiahs, but John was the first we encountered near Capernaum.

I was not rebellious. I had little knowledge of the Scriptures, and I knew the Romans were tyrants but they allowed us to practice our faith freely. Jonah taught myself and my brother the religious observances, the traditions and the festivals which we celebrated in their courtyard and in their house. I had learnt a little of these from our home in Bethsaida but we never spoke of revolt, only of the day when the Messiah would come to free us and bring in the reign of God. We had to be patient, for God worked in his own time.

Andrew was very attracted to the baptist. He spent days away with him and listened to his preaching. I was alone with the boats and nets and sometimes Zebedee would hire help for me. But I was worried, for following a preacher was dangerous and time-wasting. We had to put food in our mouths and upkeep the house and boat. I did not admonish him since he was so involved with the prophet, and came home full of words and wonder, but I could only lament. Andrew had been converted, and would leave home, and follow the baptist.

Then, while my hair and beard were still dark but with streaks of gray, Jonah brought word from the village of a good woman he thought would make a suitable wife—she was his niece. He acted on my behalf and talked to his brother. I must admit I was lonely and had many days and nights when I wished for intimate company, and so I agreed to meet with them.

Zebedee gave gifts and money to his brother's family on my behalf, and they spoke together. I agreed to marry their daughter and took her a gift of a cypress chest which I had made with a donation from Zebedee, which she accepted. So, we were betrothed, and because the house was soon ready with a table and chairs I had made as a wedding gift, we celebrated marriage in the main courtyard, and she, Joanna, moved into my home the day Andrew left to follow John.

2

YESHUA

ANDREW WAS GONE FOR ABOUT eight weeks before he returned. We welcomed him accordingly, and he sat and ate but looked weather-beaten and gaunt. He said he had followed the baptist and listened to him and assisted with the baptisms when necessary. But there was something unsettled about him. He seemed more restless than usual, disturbed, or perhaps perturbed, I don't know the word. His eyes still shone, and he breathed quickly and was excited about something and he managed to restrain himself, but he was different.

We had a little wine stored after the marriage and we drank together and Joanna made a meal of vegetables, fish, and bread, and a soup with leeks. He ate and drank thankfully. Then he told us about John and something remarkable that he had witnessed. He said John was baptizing one day near Bethany and suddenly stopped and walked from the people along the river. He seemed to be looking at and following a man walking slowly along the bank. The man was tall and bearded and dressed like an Essene, possibly, but did not acknowledge us. John then stopped and nodded and seemed satisfied, and returned to the group.

Andrew continued, "John came back to us and said to look at the lamb sent by God, referring directly to the stranger who had since disappeared. We asked what he meant. John replied he, the stranger, was to be the perfect sacrifice. John then said something about him being more powerful as he will be the one who will baptize with fire, and declared that the man was alive before he, John, was born."

Andrew told us his followers were mystified, and they were in awe of his words, but did not question him. Who could this other man be?

The man, Andrew told us, returned after two days when John, recognizing the stranger again, was suddenly distraught and went near to him and asked why he came to him. The stranger replied, "For the sake of righteousness, in accordance with the Scriptures, let it be done." John was reluctant but proceeded to baptize the man, but then unsettling events followed.

"As he baptized this man the clouds rolled over, there was rumbling like thunder in the sky and some say they heard a voice, but indistinct, others not. Some say they saw a bird descend on the man but others saw nothing. John told us he heard a voice proclaiming the man, Yeshua, to be his Son. No one else heard that said. But there was a commotion as many ran for shelter and Yeshua stood alone in the waters of baptism."

The people gathered again around John as this man Yeshua dried and clothed himself and said to Andrew and another, "You are the followers of John. Now, follow me."

I asked Andrew what he had seen and heard, and he answered nothing, just the clouds and light streaming and a sound like thunder threatening rain and some confusing movement as people were scared. But it was inspiring as the streaming light seemed to shine on Yeshua.

I looked at Andrew and he drew deep breaths. He said he loved John, but after witnessing the baptism he knew Yeshua was the one, and stayed with him all day. After that, Jesus wandered into the desert of Judea alone.

I asked Andrew what else he knew about this man. Andrew said there were followers of John who became followers of Yeshua and that Yeshua repeated the message of John, and John accepted his lower position. John said Yeshua was greater than he. Andrew said Yeshua was from Nazareth but born in Bethlehem. He was a Galilean, and had never married, although Andrew said he was related to John through his mother Mary. His father, Joseph, was a carpenter, and he was also trained in various manual skills, but had attended religious instruction and was very familiar with the Scriptures.

In fact, hearing a Scripture once, he could remember it perfectly. And Yeshua said Isaiah was the prophet to take most heed of. I asked Andrew if he called himself the Messiah; he answered no, but John did, and others called him "Yeshua-Immanuel." Then I asked Andrew why he found this Yeshua to be so compelling. And he said it was his baptism, and the fact that John had predicted his coming and that he was said by John to be greater than he, and described him as the "Lamb of God." We all understood the lamb to be a sacrifice, but in relation to Yeshua it made little sense. But Andrew said his name, Yeshua, meant "to save"; it was, however, a common name.

Andrew said Yeshua spoke with authority and urgency and never paused or stuttered. His voice was clear and calm and enticed people to listen.

That was all? I asked.

Andrew said that after about forty days he came again to John and took many of John's followers with him, and John acquiesced.

"He spoke to us and told us what had happened—that he had prayed in the wilderness before the start of his ministry to prepare himself in the spirit, and was approached by the prince of demons. Yeshua said never to be affronted by this deceitful one as he only has the power that we concede him, but be awake to him. I asked what he meant. Jesus said the great demon will try to take root in the heart while we are sleeping. And if you have let in the demon he will not leave. Or if he does, and you fall asleep again, he will return with many more. Do not fall for his flattery or false promises. Consider carefully what he says and in return rely on Scripture and the voice that God will give you."

He then said Yeshua countered the prince of demon's arguments to sin with Scripture, and the demon's words were laden with menace. He told us we should all meet evil in the same way. See it for the danger that it is, not to ignore it or accommodate it or reduce it, or think we can contain it once it has taken hold. Evil beguiles, so we must be aware and cunning, and never sleep.

Andrew continued, "I then asked him what the demon looked like. Was he deformed or monstrous? He said no, but it was his spirit that was diabolical.

"I listened to him for he spoke to us of sin and repentance with a pleading almost. He made us believe God's coming was imminent and the way must be prepared. He frightened and aroused, but always he captured attention with his insistence on repentance as the entrance to an eternal life with God, as John had also said."

"Eternal life? What did he mean?" I asked. "And who was this prince of demons?" Andrew said he never explained but said all would be revealed in time. Andrew also said he (Andrew) had left the baptist now and was a follower of Yeshua, and others did the same, but now he would stay for a while and live with us and fish as before. And he came back to us but lived with Jonah's family to allow us privacy until we built another two rooms onto the house.

That night Philip, a native also from Bethsaida who had befriended Andrew in Capernaum and also followed Yeshua, rested with us, and told us about an amazing feat that he had seen Jesus perform. At a wedding feast at Cana, he was asked by his mother to provide more wine, for the last jar had been finished. Yeshua then, not denying his mother and aware that he had brought excess guests with him, told the stewards to taste again the jars of water, and doing so, they discovered wine. And everyone complimented the host on the quality, but asked why they kept the best wine until last, and why did they keep it hidden?

Then, when word came that Yeshua was in Capernaum, Andrew and Philip left and Andrew returned some days later. He told us of strange acts performed by this man Yeshua such as healing the sick and expelling a demon from the synagogue in Galilee. The next time he went with Jesus to Jerusalem with a few others and there he later told me how Jesus violently chased the money changers out of the temple in Jerusalem. It was said he was then brought to the notice of the authorities as it caused a near riot.

Money changing was an acceptable practice in order to pay the temple tribute in shekels, not Roman coin. Did this man know what he was doing? He also told the animal sellers who were God-fearers but not Jewish to sell no more. The animals were a necessity as they were sold for personal sacrifice. But Yeshua had no time for them because he accused them of dishonesty and unfair trade, and of turning the house of God, his Father's house, into a den of thieves.

"'His Father's house?'" I asked. "But God is Father to all."

Andrew replied, "But he said if the temple was destroyed, in three days he will build it up again and that would be the testimony to his authority."

I was stunned at that. What was he talking about? Who will destroy the temple? He can rebuild it in three days? Was he mad?

John, James, and myself listened with fascination but reserve. This man was not ordinary and gathered many followers who supported him. Andrew told us more were coming to him every day, giving him alms, and women too. He never begged for anything. He was always provided for. And while in Jerusalem he met an elderly Pharisee; his name was Nicodemus, and he told the man that it was necessary to be born again in water and spirit to enter the kingdom of heaven, and the wise old man was left wondering, for he had never heard such things.

"'Born again?'" I asked.

"That's what he said," Andrew replied. "Reborn in the water and spirit. But Nicodemus did not understand what Yeshua was saying either, and Yeshua chastised him for being a teacher and not knowing these things."

I did not know what he meant, nor did James or John. We asked Andrew to clarify, but he wasn't sure either. "He said the Son of Man was the only one ever to go to heaven. I will learn more, but this man Yeshua says we must believe what he says, for he knows that way to eternal life." I asked again what this eternal life was. But Andrew shook his head and said, "Only those that believe in this man's words and repent will experience it."

A few weeks later, Andrew told us the news that the baptist had been arrested by order of Herod. I felt my brother was in danger then. The Roman authorities were repressing Zealots but John was not a Zealot. His message was peaceful and luminous, but still Herod Agrippa had him arrested.

When I questioned Andrew, he said John had often criticized Herod for marrying his brother's wife, Herodias, while his brother was still alive. There were also rumors that the marriage was incestuous and so it was condemned by Jewish law, and John, fearless, accused Herod Agrippa of unrighteousness. Probably at his wife's insistence, but also fearing a possible rebellion instigated by John, Herod had him arrested. As a result, his followers were angered and protested and Herod was reluctant to proceed with any further punishment for fear of inciting the people further.

We fished for a few days quietly and I could see Andrew was anxious to return to Yeshua and soon he would leave again, possibly never to return. I loved my brother and saw only grievance for both of us. He was lost to this man and he longed for the day he could reunite. But his service I needed, and we worked together, but with lagging spirits.

I was interested in what Andrew had said about this man Yeshua and his miracles. He said he was curing people of sicknesses in Judea with just a touch or a word. I found such stories difficult to accept, being a practical man, but Andrew was convinced he had powers stronger than magic. But from whence came his powers? Many sorcerers roamed the hills and convinced onlookers their powers were from God; but were they bespoke powers from a malignancy?

This man Yeshua raised many questions and I wished my brother to take heed, but he said such a good man could not be a source of evil. He was not bewitched but enlightened and would bring many with him along the way—some said he was with the baptizer at Qumran, others that he was trained by the Pharisees, as he could argue convincingly.

I trusted Andrew, for I knew him to be a clever and upright man who put the Scriptures before the words of charlatans. He knew John the baptizer and now he said he knew this Yeshua to be righteous and from God, as he said his powers were not his own, but from another greater than he, whom he called "Father." He said he believed Yeshua was the Messiah.

I said no more, and returned to work with many misgivings.

3

THE CALLING

ONE EVENING, AFTER RETURNING FROM the town, Andrew said there was a story circulating, originally told by a Samaritan woman, about how a stranger, a Jew, had arrived in Samaria and rested at Jacob's well. The woman, drawing water, said the man asked her for a drink, and she was amazed that a Jew should so address a Samaritan, and he told her that what he offered her was living water, so that she may never thirst again. She said she wanted to taste that water. He then told her to bring her husband and she told him she had none, and the man said she had many husbands, for she was an adulteress.

She was overwhelmed because he knew and did not condemn her and in fact forgave her, and told her one day there would be no distinction between Jew and Samaritan, only between those who lived in the spirit and those who did not. He told her to keep quiet about their meeting. But she could not restrain herself and told everyone she met in the town of the encounter and said the man said he was the Messiah, and she was overcome with emotion, both crying and laughing, as if she had been released from infamy. But some people who heard this in Capernaum were disgusted that a Jew should so talk to a Samaritan, and a loose woman at that.

Andrew and Philip both knew this man to be Jesus, as he was also known, and were in constant admiration of him. They said he just didn't recite like other teachers; he spoke words from his heart with deep conviction—but let it be known that many also distrusted him. Some say he was arrogant and spoke down to the people and saw himself as beyond the law and beyond criticism. Many followed him through curiosity, and some through suspicion, but most through love, for he was a man that drew love from people and returned it in plentitude. This practice of public love was most awkward, and uncommon, almost reprehensible outside the family.

Then, one day, not long after, word came that Jesus was coming to Capernaum again. Andrew told me that I must meet with Jesus, and he would introduce me. I was reluctant because there were more important matters. My mother-in-law had taken sick with fever and my wife tended to her in the house. The fish were few and we were in need of food. Always there was work to be done on the nets and boats, but I agreed, seeing how he was excited and expectant.

He took us to the sea but there was no one there except an old woman who told us Jesus and his followers had moved north. We walked in their wake for a long distance and, finally, saw people standing near a large spring outside of a cave, and there stood a man, looking like John, talking to a small crowd. Andrew said some of those present were his new followers, just come from Capernaum and its surrounds, as word traveled quickly. We made our way slowly through the crowd to the front and Jesus recognized Andrew and motioned him to come forward, and hugged and kissed him.

Andrew introduced me as Simon. Jesus then wished peace and health for me and my house. I suddenly bowed my head. Health for the family? Did he know? I then looked up at him and he greeted me again.

"Your name is Cephas, son of Jonah." And he smiled with his luminous eyes and put his hand on my shoulder. I told him my name was Simon, but he again said, "You will be called 'Cephas.'" And I did not contradict him again.

Then he left and his disciples followed him to a small fall where he sat and continued to teach from the grotto. Andrew was amongst them. And let it be known that Andrew was the first to be called between us.

I returned home alone, leaving Philip and Andrew together, and I fished but the catch was light. Rachael was almost delirious and the physician was even called and gave her some potent herbs, but still she remained ill. My wife attended her but she looked at me as if there was no hope. We prayed in the set pieces as we had been instructed in our Jewish faith.

Then my wife, Joanna, said that in the market there was talk of the man Jesus who had just come from Nazareth, his home town, and was rejected by the people who knew him there. She said he insulted them, saying a prophet is never recognized in his home town, and quoted both Elijah and Elisha to denounce them. Was he a false prophet? she asked. She also told of rumors in the town that Jesus did not keep holy the Sabbath and spoke out against the religious leaders. I said I knew nothing, except that, according to Andrew, he was an exceptional man in his bearing and knowledge of the Scriptures. He spoke with sincerity and deep meaning. That's all I knew. He proclaimed his word to be saving in some way.

The next day Andrew and I went together to the sea to fish saying nothing of the previous day except that Andrew called me "Cephas." The catch was very light in the morning and by the afternoon we decided to pull in our nets. As we did this, we noticed Jesus walking by the shore with some companions. Suddenly, Jesus called out to us, "When you have finished catching fish, come with me, and I will show how to fish for men." We were surprised and puzzled by this and sailed to the shore. What did he mean? But Jesus had moved on and met James and John and also Zebedee who was with them, and he said the same thing to them.

Now, John and James had not encountered Jesus before and his words had a profound effect on them. They dropped their nets and went over to him and they talked a while. We came up to them after leaving out boat and again he spoke to the four of us and wanted us to be his companions. Andrew said immediately he would follow his Master (as he called him) anywhere, and James and John wondered why he wanted them to be with him. And he told them that they would be chosen amongst the many and be favored in God's eyes. They looked at their father who raised his head, and, as a proud man, thanked the Lord for his gifts. Even as he would have to fish with hired help without his sons, he was still willing to part with them, even as he looked for another in the bushes.

After which we returned to our homes in discussion about what it meant, without Andrew. Go with him for what? To where? To be fishers of men? Andrew had already said he would go to him without hesitation in the morning, but I insisted we needed to fish, for the numbers had been so few and we were hungry, and Joanna and Rachael needed food, but the words were without conviction, since I had in some way been subjected to a calling without precedent, to something momentous, and knew what I must do, together with Andrew.

He asked me if I would come with him because Jesus had distinguished me with his own appellation, as if he knew me, already. But I insisted on a type of false pleading: how could I leave Joanna and Rachael? Then Joanna heard us speaking, and having heard of Jesus and his works and his promise that all can be forgiven if they repent, came over to me and said she would take care of my Rachael and would also come with us when she could.

She had already prepared a small pack of clothes and food. This was so surprising. I asked her how she knew, and she said from the first time she heard of this man, she understood that Andrew and I must follow him. She said again she would join us when she could. We rested for a while and we discussed what we had heard about Jesus in Cana, that he had somehow supplied the best wine in the water vats after the hosts had run out. And that many disciples had been witnesses. And how he had expelled demons and cured the sick, including the son of an official.

Then, I looked at my Rachael and she was sweating and heaving and her eyes were shut. Such a fever usually led to death. My wife said it would be any time now and then a knock came to the door, and Jesus was standing there, with Andrew, returned from the synagogue.

He was invited in and my wife bowed respectfully to him and asked him to sit on one of the chairs, but he sat on the floor. He reassured Joanna that the work they would do, as revealed to him, was for the greater good and it would be a short time and we would be together, then an extended time and we would not, and we would return from thence to eternal life. She smiled and said, "I know. Let it be done according to your will." And Jesus said not his will, but the will of the Father.

We knew not of the Father or eternal life, but after he had supped, he saw my mother-in-law in bed and stood and went over to her. He simply put his hand on her arm and asked her to get up. She awoke, and seeing him, was in awe, but he raised her up and told her to get some water, for she was thirsty. He drank too and then he left. Happiness beamed from Joanna's face because he so simply and effortlessly cured Rachael with love and grace, calmness and humility, as becoming a man appointed.

So, later in the evening, we set out to fish again with James and John and five others but the catch was meager. We set to the shore after many hours when Jesus appeared in the early morning with his following, a larger number, almost driving him into the sea, and he turned to us and asked to enter the boat. We went over to him and he climbed in and told us to go a little from the shore where he preached to the people from the boat.

He spoke of a kingdom of heaven and that only the just and merciful and repentant could enter. He then said the kingdom was at hand and that they would be the first to enter, not the Pharisees and Sadducees and all those who say one thing and do another, those who knew the law but never practiced it and persecuted others for the same offense they committed, but the poor and weary and downtrodden, the meek and humble who were true in spirit would be welcomed.

This was hard to understand since we all knew there were prostitutes and tax collectors and even swindlers standing and listening, but the call to repentance was not lost, but not well understood either, the way he said it. He said those who are forgiven much are truly thankful in their allegiance.

How does one repent? Only through sacrifice, as we were taught. Atonement through the sacrifice of a lamb or oxen. Was this Jesus telling us that he could forgive sins? Were we mostly so sinful, anyway? Was it our greed? Our envy? Lust? Pride? We knew of some sneaky fellows in the market but it was seen as all in a day's work. The women covered themselves; maybe they gossiped a little; we were not proud but humble workers; there were rich people in the town but we were not overly envious. Did a slight transgression constitute such great offense to God that we all needed to fall down in continual repentance to be favored in his eyes?

We could see Jesus was a great teacher but what he taught did not sit right with our learning of the law. He preached the Scriptures anew and we wanted to hear more because of the new light that he shone on them. He was offering something fresh, but was it outside the law?

Then Jesus said to go into deeper water where we will catch many fish. I protested that we had been fishing all night and were tired, but he did not reply, just signaled to push out further and to the right side of the boat drop our nets. And so, Andrew and I lowered our nets, and suddenly fish splashed in the sea, and we could not contain our nets which were full. Fish jumped onto the boat and our nets strained and started to break. I called to the others to help us and they saw what was happening and pushed out, and their nets and boat too were filled.

I turned to this man Jesus and said, following Andrew, "Master, I do not know the law and I do not keep holy and observe what I should; I am a simple man, sinful, therefore, do not waste time with me."

Jesus put his hand on my shoulder and remained standing, and asked to be taken to shore. He said he understood my reluctance to leave my livelihood and family, but these things were not as important as the mission that he would give me, and the duty I must fulfill. With that I jumped into the sea, as I was not wont to do, and helped to pull the boat to shore.

"Peter, James, John and Andrew. I call you this day to be servants of the Lord, and leaders of men. Come with me." He said this once we were on the shore. I covered myself with my garments, and we attested to our intention to follow him, as Philip and Andrew had already done.

He said he would see us again tomorrow, and not to be afraid. Then Zebedee invited Jesus to stay with him that night, and he accepted, after completing his ministry that day.

4

THE GATHERING STORM

AND SO, IN THE MORNING, with many disciples milling, Andrew, James, John, Philip, myself, and others set out with Jesus. We walked briskly together behind him and spoke little but sometimes he would make a remark and we listened and kept his words safe. Many followed and talked together in groups. Some joined him and others fell away. John and Andrew remained close; James and I, a little way back. They wanted to walk with him, and a few kept by his side all the way to the sea and surrounds.

On the way he stopped to talk to a group of villagers, and helped a leper become clean through some mystical power. The leper was fully clothed and spoke from behind his face cover, but first Jesus led him to a private yard where I and Andrew followed, and the man spoke to him and asked if Jesus could heal him. Jesus said he could and he touched him, the man looked at his hands, and they were healed. We were astounded that he should touch a leper for it was forbidden, let alone heal him. And how was it done? How severely was the man afflicted? How long had he been stricken? We wondered at these signs.

Jesus told him not to tell anyone but to present to the priests and follow the cleansing ritual as commanded by the law. In defiance, the man told everyone waiting and the word spread again, and many lepers came to ask him, but Jesus did not heal them all.

This we could not understand. Why some and not others?

But he was so well known now the crowds became overbearing wherever he went and Jesus would hide away a while from them but usually he took us with him. He sat and rested in a narrow, shaded alley. It was strange to see a man with such power fatigued, but he took water and a little bread and slept. Then there was word that Pharisees and lawyers from Judea and even Jerusalem were making their way to Galilee to investigate Jesus.

His name was known throughout the land already and his miracles were perplexing and daunting. This was no ordinary man. This was no false prophet or magician the crowds that came to him were beholding. Some were frightened, and their fear bred anxiety, and some even despised him; others were just curious. They asked, how could it be? From whence came was his power? Who was this man that Nazareth, his home town, had denied and rejected? Was he superior to the law and the Pharisees? Even Moses?

We never spoke to him of what we heard, but we were sure he was well aware. He was sometimes melancholic, and looking out to the mountains or sea, seemed always alone. He said we must leave Galilee and return to Capernaum, and many followed him on his journey. On the way they presented him with food and drink and we occasionally rested, and ate also.

In Capernaum word arrived before we did, and many were waiting and they gave us sustenance. He was immediately taken into a neighbor's house where he rested, however, a disturbance outside ensued and it was said a man who could not walk was brought to him to be healed, but he could not get near to Jesus.

Suddenly, the roof of the house was parted and a man on a stretcher was lifted down to the floor to Jesus. Jesus simply said, "Your sins are forgiven. Take up your bed and walk." The man sat up and the people gasped, and then he moved his legs and with the help of some, he stood, and still with their help he walked past Jesus and out onto the road where many waited. It was passed around that Jesus had blasphemed in the house, and some ran away in fear.

The Pharisees who had just arrived from afar spoke to each other about him after the excitement quelled. Jesus saw them with their backs turned and spoke up: "I know what you are thinking: only God can forgive sins. Therefore, I tell you, I must have authority to do such a thing. I can say 'take up your mat and walk' because the man is free from sin." He explained to us later how sickness was not sin, but sin was sickness.

They did not reply then but kept to their contention that Jesus was blasphemous as was suspected, and was declaring himself to be from God. From thence we knew that Jesus was sealing his own fate, since the Pharisees guarded their own self-righteous position and privileges fiercely. They considered themselves the nearest to God but did not have the power of Jesus and so ridiculed him as a pretender. And we realized then we were tying our fate to his by association. I invited him back to my home for supper, and he agreed.

He spoke kindly to my wife and Rachael, and they served him with fish and vegetables and a little wine, which he rejected. After a while I asked him why he said sickness was not sin when we all knew that sickness was a punishment for sin. He told us God does not punish with sickness, and sin is truly a sickness of the spirit.

He slept on the floor and refused a bed. When all was quiet, I told my wife of what had passed and she said she had heard already and was concerned, for the Pharisees and the Herodians and lawyers and priests were in the city from as far as Jerusalem. She cautioned us and held her hand to my face and we embraced, as the same ominous images passed before us.

Andrew stayed with us, and the other disciples made bed in the grounds of Zebedee.

In the morning, we returned to the city with Jesus and as usual crowds gathered in groups looking and chatting. We walked with him and ignored some taunts, but there were also praises. Jesus surprisingly went up to a tax collector in the center of town and, refusing to pay the tax he asked, as he already paid, stood face-to-face with the tax collector and told him warmly and sincerely to be his disciple.

The man, named Matthew, stood dismayed and looked at his ill-gotten coin and then recognized Jesus, as he had heard of him, and had seen him in the streets. He was amazed as Jesus had spoken to him, a tax collector, and he willingly and humbly accepted the invitation and the command to join him. The man discarded the coin, closed his books, and immediately came with us.

The townspeople were disgusted that he should talk to such a man let alone ask him to follow him. Such a man was of the lowest caste, an outcast, a swindler and betrayer, a Roman sycophant, and a traitor to his people.

Andrew and I were also stunned and could not see why Jesus chose him. It was difficult to accept. It made us feel devalued; we were fishermen but honest, and it would draw anger from the people. But Matthew came along with the disciples and we greeted and welcomed him as best we could. Matthew then invited Jesus to rest and refresh. Jesus agreed, and Matthew took a few of us to a tavern he said he owned, for he was wealthy from the taxes, and we were seated, and food and wine was brought to us.

We saw that some of Matthew's friends, the publicans, were also there, and also some women who wandered the streets, and other people considered undesirable, such as robbers, by reputation.

At first, I was not comfortable, but with the food and drink and atmosphere we relaxed and found the company warm and friendly and the food replenishing. Of course, some Pharisees, who were following and detailing us now, later reproved Jesus for associating with the unclean, but he always responded directly and with force, for the Pharisees were reprehensible in their closed attitude and stubborn ways. Jesus told them, "The healthy have no need of a physician. I have come to heal the sick." He then told how the sacrifice of the self-righteous was not as desirous as alms from the poor, as acts of repentance. For in God's eyes, the love of a fellow man is beyond sacrifice and is the same as love for God himself.

But worse still, some disciples of John the baptist who were with us even questioned Jesus on why he celebrated and did not fast. Jesus said there would be time for fasting but they were celebrating together as was appropriate at the moment. He compared the moment to a wedding feast and how it was proper to celebrate with the groom while he was still with them.

He then remarked how the time for new wine to be poured into new skins had arrived. We were not sure what he meant again—whether referring to John's disciples or the Pharisees. But we took it to mean that his words were the new wine.

Having convinced them of nothing, the Pharisees resented what he said, as an insult to them and to the Scriptures, and to God, as they took Jesus to mean they were the old garments and old skins. And they despised him because he broke with tradition and the law, deliberately. But he did not say the old skins or garments should be abandoned; indeed, it would be a loss if they were torn or broken, as we understood him.

After that, Jesus spent the day preaching and we sat and listened, but few asked any questions; they either accepted or rejected what he said, they were offended or pleased, but among themselves they debated and questioned.

At the end of the day Jesus told us he would go to Jerusalem, which was a long and difficult journey. Some would go with him, including Andrew, James, and John, but I said I would go home to Joanna, and he said nothing but brushed past me and said he would return after the Passover.

5

The New Law

When I was at home, Joanna had already heard of the man with palsy and the damage to the roof. She had also heard of the Pharisees' resentment of Jesus and his disciples, among whom she now counted me. She worried for us and said the Pharisees would not tolerate abuse of their authority and that they were already set against him. Jesus did not handle them properly and was purposefully provoking them. She said, "Why aggravate them? Can't Jesus work without insulting them? I know he does marvelous things, but the man is troublesome. Look at the baptist, and he only annoyed Herod once. They are watching Jesus too, especially the Herodians."

I agreed with her but told her Jesus was more than a healer. He spoke about his mission to save sinners. She replied that wasn't his doing—to save. He must not contravene the Scriptures or put himself at odds with the priests and religious. It will be his undoing, and all who walk with him. Why was he so confrontational?

I said that was his way. He did not hold back when he saw error or corruption; he spoke out against it. He hated the attitude of the Sadducees and Pharisees. He thought they were worse than sinners, and they paraded as righteous. And then she asked why I had eaten with sinners. I told her they were the people Jesus had come to help, to bring them out of their destitution, to give them hope, whereas the Pharisees banished them. She said he went about it the wrong way, and the people in the town were turning against him.

Then three women friends of Joanna's came to visit. They sat and talked of Jesus and praised him, but Joanna was cautious and checked outside, and they continued. They took some tea and one woman named Susanna, and another Salome, said they had followed him all day listening and witnessing and they provided money for his repast, and they then sang songs and recited the psalms and were happy, smiling, free-spirited, above anything I had seen before.

Joanna was a follower? "Joanna?" I asked in surprise. Joanna looked at me and smiled and she said she was happy I was home, but never to leave Jesus again. She honored him also, together with the wife of Zebedee, and her face and mood were suddenly soaked in an avid devotion. I asked why she spoke against him. She answered, "I did not speak against him, but in defense and support, and to make you aware."

Jesus returned to Galilee, and all the time news of his works came to us, and the women met together and spoke almost every night, and more came and brought their husbands also; there were soon too many, so Zebedee suggested enlarging the house, changing its room appointments, which we proceeded to do when we had time.

Husbands came and helped with the extension of the house which was soon large enough for many to come and talk and sing and share drinks and discuss his words. Even the shape of the house was changed to octagonal so people could sit and talk together, and more bedrooms were added. But it was the women who wept when they spoke of him, wept with happiness and grief, and as some were wealthy, they agreed to support his ministry, including Joanna, as much as she could be with him.

As well as the good news there was also some worrying news. Jesus had been charged with violating the Sabbath while in Jerusalem by curing a sick man and declaring his Father was God. This troubled everyone, for the Sabbath was holy and to say you are God's Son was the same as to say you were God. Surely, this is not what he meant. But in Jerusalem, he could not be ignored. And he could not make the Pharisees and Sadducees look unholy, it was demeaning not only to them, but to all Jews.

Word came that Jesus was returning, and we went again to meet him at Capernaum. Many hundreds gathered and called out to him when they saw him, but many were also silent. I joined Andrew and James and the others and we walked together and Andrew told me of the happenings in Jerusalem and that the authorities were wanting to arrest him, but he had such a following, they dared not.

We walked some way together in a field of corn and Jesus told us we could take some ears and we squashed them and ate. It was the Sabbath and

I told Jesus, but he said, "You are hungry, then eat. The Sabbath was made for men." And we were followed by the Pharisees who immediately scolded us. As well they asked if we had permission to take the corn. And Jesus said the Pharisees always broke the Sabbath and it was attested in the Scriptures that when one is hungry, one must eat.

I was apprehensive because to say that the Sabbath was made for men was like saying all the laws were made for men and were from men, whereas we were taught that the law preceded man. Was Jesus denying that right and wrong, the very law we upheld, was fixed by God?

With that he left us and returned to town. We followed soon after and the scene was repeated when Jesus cured an artisan with a withered hand who was ashamed of begging. Jesus cured him, and immediately, the Pharisees, waiting in the synagogue, came to him and asked if it was sinful to work on the Sabbath. Jesus simply replied that it was always lawful to do good. And I could see the Pharisees hardened in their hearts and their faces turned to stone, embarrassed by their inability to catch him out and by his innuendoes. Besides, he said again, how often do the Pharisees ignore the Sabbath?

As we left, I could see the Pharisees mingling with the Herodians in the city, joined in anger and spite.

He preached during the afternoon outside Capernaum near the sea and then at twilight took us to a small mountain where he said he would spend the night. Some women brought nuts and lentils and water from the village and I recognized two of them from the house. Jesus left us and walked further up the mountain to be alone, and we talked a little together before we slept.

There were many disciples there, and we waited for him until the morning. Matthew asked me about the miracles. "How does he do them?" I told him I had heard of magicians who could heal, and it wasn't so surprising. "But you saw with your own eyes," he said. "Do you doubt him?" The miracles were wonders, but not what put him above the others. I said his words do not deceive; they are mixed with scorn and love, and instruction and criticism, and deep understanding, intrigue, and they were the sign of his mission amongst us. The miracles will be weighed by those who have not seen, but his words are to be honored and upheld.

Matthew was satisfied, but concerned that I did not accept Jesus' powers fully. But I assured him that the powers he had were not his, as he had told us many times, and so saying, he was authenticated. The power came from another, higher authority. "Is it from God?" Matthew asked. I told him I didn't know, as he had more to tell us, and the baptist had ordained him, but I knew Jesus spoke in riddles at times to confuse those who looked to repudiate him, and he would always explain his meaning to us.

In the morning, Jesus came down from the mountain and gathered twelve of us together and named me Peter (not Simon or Cephas), my brother Andrew, the sons of Zebedee—John and James—Philip, Bartholomew, Matthew, Thomas, James (son of Alpheus), Simon known as the Zealot, Judas (son of James) and Judas Iscariot. I knew James (son of Alpheus), Simon the Zealot, and the two Judases in passing only. Jesus said we would be his constant companions.

He then said strange things to us, saying that God's kingdom is for the poor. What did he mean by "God's kingdom?" And who were "the poor?" Weren't we all poor? And didn't the wealthy women provide for him? He said in the kingdom all things would be reversed, the poor will be rich, the sad happy, the hungry satisfied.

He went further and told us we will be mocked and sworn at for following him, but that we must be happy at that for even the prophets were scorned. But then he turned to the gathered crowd and said the most remarkable things. He said to love your enemies. To be kind to those who hurt you. Give to those who ask. Turn the other cheek when struck, and be merciful.

He could see we were taken aback, and spoke further still, and said to give to all who ask and do not look for a reward. I turned to Matthew—he was uneasy too, eyes lowered. We couldn't believe what we were hearing. Do not fight for what was lawfully ours, but to give it all away? Never to judge another? This was not how God acted or what he expected, surely.

We knew about doing unto others as you would have them do unto you, but it was never emphasized the way Jesus stated it, as the forefront of his teaching.

These were not entirely the teachings of the Scriptures. Do not criticize or condemn others? Didn't the Scriptures say a wicked man is condemned and vengeance is the Lord's? Didn't the Lord say he would smite our enemies? And how to forgive without retribution? Forgiveness was from God, not from man. We had to take what was ours and protect it, surely. I looked to James and he was silent also. How would it be possible to preach this message to Jews in the towns and villages? Who would listen? Strive to be perfect? Who can be perfect?

It was impossible. His message was so counter to our teachings and traditions. Was this the Messiah, the man who said do not go to war with your enemies? How then was Israel to be liberated? Were enemies made to be loved? Blessed are the weak and supine? The peacemakers were blessed? Was he elevating acceptance of tyranny? Blessed are those who let life wash over them without struggle? The meaning wasn't clear to us at all then. Perhaps understanding would follow.

He said that looking curiously and even unconsciously at a woman was akin to adultery. The thought and the act were the same, even when there was no material deprivation or hurt? That was the measure by which we applied the law. So, what made condemnation warranted? Were we to be persecuted and condemned for all our thoughts, some of which passed unnoticed? The law said "do not covet thy neighbor's wife or goods" but in the litany of misdeeds they were considered of secondary importance. I wondered if it was possible to be pure in heart and yet evil in action? Or pure in action, yet evil in heart, as he said?

Many things fought in my head, and he spoke on and on, each word more disturbing than the last. And then, finally, he said his words were the sure foundations of spiritual strength, which was always wavering if built on coercive laws, but constructed on love and generosity and mercy, they can never fail. As I understood it, the Mosaic law prescribed what was not to be done—his law told us what must be done. And finally, he told us not to care about anything except one's spirit, which must be cleansed from evil through sincere repentance.

Then there was a message from the town at Capernaum that a good God-fearing centurion who loved the people and had built the synagogue there was in need of Jesus to cure his servant. Jesus made his way to the town and we followed, but the centurion, on meeting Jesus, would not let him enter his house as he considered himself unworthy, even though he had put himself in danger by summoning the healer. Impressed with the centurion's faith, the servant was cured. He then said many would come from all areas far and wide and be welcomed to the table, and many who were already in the Lord's house will be thrown out.

Again, his reference to the prophesized elect, or the remnant, or even the Pharisees was evident, and they were obviously filled with anger as they listened. They, the Pharisees and priests, still followed him and listened and held consul about him.

Jesus retired with us to my house for the evening and welcomed the women who came to be with him. They ate together and he talked to them and they listened and they wanted him to stay and not to leave, but in the morning, he said we would return to Galilee, and they insisted they would go with him.

He told me my new house had many rooms now, and it was good to be here, and before he retired, he looked at me and asked why I was so silent. I said it was because there were many to honor him, especially the women, and I had little time to be close to him. He said the women were disciples too, as God did not differentiate, and the kingdom of God belongs to all with faith, and to be content, as I was especially chosen.

I was satisfied and lay my head on the straw, questions unabated, watching him as the puzzles drifted into dreams.

6

THE PARABLES

AS HE SAID, THE NEXT DAY Jesus set out for Galilee again, rising very early and eating nuts and fruit left for him. There were many wanting to follow him from Capernaum, waiting, and some came from their houses when they heard he was leaving. The women from my house followed him, but Joanna stayed back. We traveled to Galilee, and then to Nain.

He traveled for days and crowds greeted him outside of Nain. As always, they waited for his words. He told them to do good to one another, to forgive each other, to love one another, to put behind them wrongs of the past, and to judge not: for as we judge others, so will we be judged.

They asked, "How does he know how God judges? God taught us to despise our enemies." He told them, "God is perfect, and he lets the rain fall on the good and the evildoers. By your good deeds, others will know you, and you will be rewarded in heaven where your treasure is stored."

There were still many questions people harbored and Jesus grew tired and finally he taught them how to pray. Not with many set words and incantations and repetitions, but from the heart; to be thankful and forgiving and simple. "Pray in private; fast in private; do not worry about the future; as children of the Father you are provided for; be better than the Pharisees, for they parade their hollowness." This was difficult since public sacrifice and penance were meant to show others you were a righteous and a keeper of the law. Was he saying it didn't matter what others thought about you? But it did matter.

Then we traveled on to Nain where Jesus performed an amazing miracle. It was hard to believe, even witnessing as we did. During the day we received some disciples who had come from John the baptist who was imprisoned in Machaerus in Jordan, and they delivered a message from him asking if Jesus was the anointed one, or should they wait for another.

Then Jesus performed this miracle by raising a boy who was said to be dead to life. He had heard the pleas of his mother, a widow, and took pity on her and held the boy's hand and spoke to him and he opened his eyes and sat up upon the funeral pallet. After that, Jesus replied to the disciples to tell John everything they had seen and heard, and that he was the Messiah.

He also said that John was the greatest of the prophets and those baptized by him were in front of all others. The Pharisees, aware that they had not been baptized, again resented Jesus for his deliberate denunciation.

The news of the raising spread and even his disciples were stupefied and did not know how to receive it. Who was this man? He was flesh and blood but how could he be from God? Is God of flesh and blood? He gets hungry and tired and is hated by the priests and Pharisees, yet he does not simply repeat the Scriptures but shows how they should be understood, and after hundreds of years, how they had been neglected, despite their mindless recitation.

But in praise or disbelief, Jesus was celebrated wherever he went, awaited and listened to.

After leaving Nain, Jesus walked on many days to Magdala in Judea, preaching and teaching along the way. We always walked and sat near him, attended to him, but it was the women who provided for his needs. They kept him fed, clothed, washed, and housed. They also provided for us, his apostles, when they could, by renting a large house or preparing a banquet ahead of our arrival. Often the people let us in without charge, for they had great admiration for the prophet and his followers.

He preached all morning in Magdala and then at midday, a Pharisee, Simon, welcomed Jesus to his home for rest and a meal. Jesus accepted, and while we took ourselves outside and ate food away from the women, Jesus went with Simon's servant. We were not surprised that a Pharisee such as Simon had approached Jesus because we had heard that some of them were interested in his lectures and debated with him openly and trustingly in the synagogues; even when he was a child it was said he debated with the Pharisees, and they were surprised at his learning.

This Pharisee, Simon, had long heard of Jesus and wanted not to debate but treat him as he deserved, for he knew he was a prophet. Not all priests were of the same cloth, as Jesus well knew, as were not all Romans or Jews. He gratefully accepted, and after we had eaten and rested, Andrew and I went to the house and saw Jesus reclining next to the table. He was having his feet washed and kissed by a woman. More so, she dried his feet with her hair.

There were some disciples with him and as she poured expensive perfume on him, they protested that the perfume should not be wasted but sold and given to the poor. What really affronted them was the woman washing his feet. Jesus rebuffed them and said that he would not always be with them and they should cherish the moment, because what she did was a beautiful gesture. Simon the Pharisee, however, knew she was an immoral woman, and watching her kiss his feet many times, crying and wiping them, became withdrawn. Nor was the scene edifying for any of us.

Jesus looked at him and said simply that the act was acknowledged as a preparation for his burial, and because she had sinned much and was forgiven, much was given back in love. The Pharisee could see Jesus was well aware, and he was so much affected by the anointing that he said it would be remembered always when other acts were forgotten, and so he let it rest, but it was still unsettling.

So far, we had avoided any hint of scandal, always keeping the sleeping quarters separated, and Jesus usually slept alone. Any hint of impropriety would be condemnation but Jesus saw it differently. Any act of charity or love earned commendation.

For the rest of the day Jesus preached, and when he saw that many who were listening were wealthy as they were well dressed and had servants, he told them that no one can serve two masters—God and money. He said everything is passing, so why store up riches which will rot away in time? Store up credit in heaven where your treasure is safe. He told them God will provide because he knew what they needed, and that pagans care about appearances and the future in terms of investments, and do not live happily because of their worry. He told them to live for the day in righteousness and let tomorrow take care of itself. Again, it was counter to the law as we were taught it.

There was, I noticed then, one woman who was unusually close to Jesus. She sat and walked with him so we could not get near, and she gave him food which he took. I thought it was the sinner from Simon's house, but it was not her. This woman was obviously wealthy by her clothing and jewelry and her hair was covered and her movements were refined, and Jesus encouraged her. She was confident with him, as if she had always known him, and he with her. I asked Thomas if he knew her and he said she was Mary from Magdala, and had just become a disciple.

That night after supper, the twelve whom Jesus had chosen sat together in the tavern and we drank a little without him. I wanted to talk about the women who were following Jesus. The meal was paid for by them. I asked was it good to have so many women followers and to be dependent on them? They did not respond except to say that Jesus knew his own. I asked was it considered decent conversing with them openly in public in such a familiar way?

Women had always been seen, culturally, as a corrupting influence and we asked each other why Jesus acknowledged them publicly and allowed them to do things for him that were strictly improper. I also complained that they surrounded him and we could not get close to him anymore. And James, too, had earlier agreed that the women were too close and brought scorn upon all of us.

Philip asked why I worried about the women. "Do they harm you?" I answered that Jesus had enough to contend with as the priests and the authorities accused him of the breach of tradition, and even of the law. Why bring criticism more upon himself? Jesus said divorcing a woman forces her to commit adultery. Is this right? No one answered. He said a man that looks at a woman should tear his eyes out. Is he serious? For self-harm was uncompromisingly condemned by the law. He travels close to these women and talks to them in public; is it seemly? They could harm him more by their love; that was my concern, and they should be discreet.

Philip replied that if the Master thought it was proper, even if it was meant to be provocative, then we need not worry, and that I was too concerned about appearances, which was, actually, far from the truth. I thought how people would misinterpret what they saw and bring derision.

The next day I sought out Jesus and I found him in a secluded place speaking closely with Mary again, and she was crying, and he hugged her with great tenderness. I saw this happen several times when they were alone at various places and she was, each time, more splendid in her appearance, more loving and devoted, renewed by her grief. At least it was fairly private and not a public display.

That same day we returned to Capernaum and I to my home to greet Joanna. She told me the faithful gathered every night in the home and spoke about him and sang songs and were joyous like a family celebrating together. But I told her of the incident in Simon the Pharisee's house and

I told her of the woman, Mary from Magdala. She asked why I thought it improper. I said being a woman, she should know. But then Joanna stood and wrapped her shawl over her head and came close to me. "Don't you understand, Peter? These women are his family also—his sisters and mother and nieces. It's the love of God's family that moves him, and the family are those who listen to him and believe, and it his mission to gather that family that they might find God, and peace with each other. Is it unseemly to hug and kiss your mother or sister?"

I told her it just opened up more ground for adversity, as his opponents did not understand. But I was moved by her words, and said I would not question it again.

The next day we met in Capernaum and Jesus was surrounded by people and his disciples, and he was asked to cure a man both blind and mute. He did so with a touch. The people were again enthralled but still they asked more in acceptance than skepticism, "Is this the Messiah? The son of David that we were promised?" And the Pharisees were told what people were saying and were asked the same questions, and they fiercely rebuked the people. They proclaimed that only Beelzebub can cast out devils, and the people agreed with them.

Jesus heard them and took their point and turned it against them. "By whom did your prophets cast them out?" But still the people refused to believe and listened to the Pharisees, and Jesus told them to look with their own eyes and see what they have seen: with the touch of a finger the kingdom of God has come.

Then he left, and we followed him, but many remained behind. He took us to the sea where crowds surrounded him, and again Mary was close to him and sat near his feet. And he preached in parables which appealed to many, some more than others. Some were left wondering, but then for others the parables gave them insights and left them convinced of his truth and validity. No one who heard him was left untouched.

All his parables were centered on the New kingdom, and always they asked, "What must I do to enter the kingdom of heaven?," or "What is the kingdom like?" They were curious and not always accepting, especially when his words seemed to contravene what they had been taught. It wasn't that they were stubborn, but they found it difficult to put what he told them above their tradition, or the teachings of their elders, or those learned in the Scriptures.

On this day he sat on a boat with the permission of the owner, who was a disciple, and told the crowd what heaven was like; he told them four parables and together he claimed that the day of reckoning will come soon, and the separation of the faithful and the evil ones will take place on that day. He also told them that his word is like a mustard seed or unleavened bread which when planted or mixed with yeast will rise far beyond its humble beginnings, and in multitude. Lastly he told a parable of a farmer who spread seeds over his field but only some of the seeds were productive.

When he was finished, he dispersed the crowds and we remained with him, and he told us three more parables in which heaven is likened to a great treasure which when one finds it, and realizes its value, sells everything to keep it.

That night we discussed the parables and saw that the word of God was to be spread and that we should sow the seed in time, and that the word would become dominant and although spread far and wide many will still not heed, but others would hear and believe. And so, from a simple sermon by a Galilean by the lake, the kingdom of God's people rested and would grow and be entered by those who could see the truth and value in what had been revealed.

Mary asked us one night after prayer if we valued what we had discovered. Would we sacrifice everything for the riches of heaven? We all agreed without question, but we could see the hardships for many of his followers, for their lives were guided by the Scriptures and tradition and custom, and they were comfortable with that which had been passed from generations and were not looking for a religious upheaval. To uproot themselves from family and work and turn against each other in pursuance of a parable of an itinerant teacher was problematic for some, impossible for most.

If people rejected Jesus, surely many would cast us out too, I said. He has the authority of heaven and still they reject him. But then Mary assured us that Jesus had not finished his ministry and he would give us the power to do what he had done and give us the eloquence to preach as he preaches, as there was much more to learn from him. In his parable of the sower, he already saw that many would not reach maturity in the Lord, and forfeit heaven.

We were surprised by her confidence. But I wondered why the farmer wasn't more careful about where he spread his seeds, looking only to the fertile soil. Mary again rose and said what farmer can afford the time to be so exacting? The wind and birds take the seed and what looks fertile may be barren, and barren, fertile. And there are many fields to sow.

We were again corrected by a woman, and increasingly so. She had insights, and I recalled this woman, Mary, hugging and kissing and crying during those times together with Jesus. Did Jesus favor the women and divulge meanings where he kept them from us? James agreed we should be given more contact with him. John, however, told us to be calm, he was only one man, and he had favored us greatly.

Then, suddenly, on the floor, I found myself standing between two women, Mary and another. I quickly moved to the opposite side. Mary saw me and understood. "The day will come, Simon Peter, when the status of your position in a room amongst the community will have no bearing."

The women left us for the night and we wondered what tomorrow would bring as Jesus wanted to cross the sea, to the east shore, and perhaps return to Nazareth. The Nazarenes had been the less supportive of Jesus, and we were to understand why soon enough.

James, brother of John, spoke up about things that troubled him. He said they were taught by their parents and their parents that there were seven kingdoms. Of which did Jesus speak? Was it the seventh heaven? Was he saying men could reside with the throne of God and all the seraphim, cherubim, and hayyoth? Or was he preaching the eternal life of the Egyptians? Or was it the return to the garden of Eden? He talks of judgment. Is the heart to be judged as in old Egypt? The Grecian Jews—those who could speak Greek and had been influenced by Greek culture—had taught us about such things from the past, but we had remained faithful to the Scriptures.

It seemed a direct assault on Jesus' teaching by James, and Simon, known as the Zealot, did not abstain. He said the day would come when we must choose between the Scriptures and the Master's teachings. But I replied that he had told us he had come to fulfill the Scriptures, not to reject them. And yet, James said, Jesus preached an afterlife as the most important aspect of living and not the importance of life on earth, as the Scriptures taught.

Simon said he had heard that the Essenes believed in a spirit within us that leaves the body at death, which we knew to be the belief of the Hellenes, as well as Persians and Egyptians. He also said, however, that Jesus was a new-age prophet who would release us from bondage, and was not a slave to the Romans, the Pharisees, or the law, but he was truly free. He said he followed Jesus to discover true freedom through him but was not in favor of abandoning the law.

We rested then, but not one of us succumbed to our doubts enough to leave him. John, in particular, wept quietly, and we slept in peace, so that in the morning we may relive our faith, for each morning it is born anew.

7

GALILEE AND BEYOND

WE STARTED EARLY AND JESUS again made his way to the sea, followed by
crowds of followers jostling and talking excitedly. The women came with us
carrying water and food. Matthew thought we might ask followers for alms
after Jesus preached to them, but the opinion was that Jesus was given all
that he needed from his disciples and the women. To me, I agreed and said I
would ask Jesus if we could make a collection from the people in the future.

We were very tired from the day before and even Jesus stopped many
times. However, we reached the sea by the afternoon and we rented a boat
for the crossing. He took only the twelve he had chosen with him and told
the others he would return when he was finished with his mission in Galilee.

So, we set sail and the weather was dull and overcast and thunder
rolled across the darkened sky and low clouds scampered above us like
chased demons. And what awaited us was preempted by these scenes. A
terrible storm blew up and the sea turned wild as it sometimes did, and
threw the boat about, and we thought it would sink, and we awakened Jesus
from his sleep, and then the storm quelled as he spoke, or after he spoke it
did not seem so terrible, I'm not sure which. "Did you think I would let you
drown? What does it take to convince you?"

And by morning we had a safe passage to the east bank in the land of
the Gerasene. Again, we were astounded at his authority. John said he had
no more need of evidence and said to the Lord that he did not fear; he was
a believer and gave his heart completely, and the Lord responded in kind,
wrapping John in his cloak and keeping him close always, with a kind look

and gentle words. John was the youngest of us, and favored also by the women.

We walked a little up the banks to the grass on the rise when suddenly came two fugitives from the caves near the embankment, naked and screaming—they were restrained, but fiercely strong. The demons that possessed them recognized Jesus, and asked why he had come—to torment them? I stood in front of Jesus as did James, but Jesus did not flinch.

Calmly, he asked them their names, and the demons spoke through the mouths of the men: "We are Legion." Then they succumbed and exclaimed, "Do not expel us. If you must, let us enter the pigs." For there was a herd of many pigs nearby, and Jesus did as they asked, and the spirits entered the pigs, and they jumped off the cliff into the sea. It was hard to accept what we saw.

Strangely, the two men were then aware of their nakedness and asked for clothes. We gave them some of our own and they dressed properly and were covered. Jesus refused permission for the men to follow him but told them to tell others in Gerasene, and to spread the word throughout the Decapolis. The herder of the pigs was incensed, however. He rushed off to the town and many came to Jesus as he walked and told him to stay away from them. They called out to him, pleading for him to go away, some abusing him, for he would bring both God's wrath, as well as the Romans.

And we told them that Jesus had come to offer salvation but they rejected him, and we were angry at their ingratitude, and James raised his voice against their abuse, saying they would be the first to be destroyed, but Jesus told him to refrain because many would not recognize him and would reject his offer of salvation, and to move on as their reckoning was coming.

Shortly, we returned to Capernaum, as we were not welcomed in Gerasene. We told the townspeople of the curing of the demoniacs and the hostility of the town. Mary said the people were frightened of him, and it was to be expected.

A messenger then came to Jesus saying that the ruler of the synagogue's daughter was near death and asked for her to be healed. He headed for Jarius' house, but on the way, Jesus suddenly stopped and asked who had touched the hem of his cloak. No one answered but he seemed to know, and looked at one woman who fell at his feet saying, "I was bleeding and unclean for twelve years, but now I'm healed." He answered, "Your faith, and not the fringe of my cloak, has cured you."

When we arrived at Jairus' house Jesus ordered everyone out. There was anguish and crying for they said she was already dead. Jesus rebuked the hysteria, and with John, James, and myself, went over to the young girl and asked her to get up, and she obeyed. I looked to James; he showed surprise, and a little fear. We understood the importance of an only child and Jesus had shown no discrimination in curing a young girl. Was she only asleep, as he maintained? She lay wane and motionless but when she arose, she ate some bread as if she had been sleeping.

Jesus asked the parents to not tell of what happened, but news spread quickly anyway, and it was soon well known throughout Galilee. But why did Jesus want the signs of his ministry not known? Some miracles he healed publicly, but others he wanted kept quiet. I asked Matthew and John, and Matthew said Jesus never boasted about his powers. He never said, "Look, see what I can do? I can bring people back to life," but he was afraid that his powers would be seen as a corruption or vanity or perhaps the people would become insensitive to his workings as a kind of rehearsed magic. But I thought it was because he did not need any affirmation from anyone, only his heavenly Father. But the truth always leaked and people who promised to remain silent were so overcome they could not restrain themselves.

Jesus then said we were going to Nazareth. His disciples would follow. I asked why Nazareth, since the last visit he was not welcomed there. But he insisted that Nazareth would turn and his home and family would accept him as the news of his authority reached them. He wanted Nazareth to believe, and be saved. James and myself thought otherwise. Andrew simply said that we do not question his judgment, for he sees what cannot be seen.

As we walked, we saw John and Mary close to Jesus and many women came with us and gave us water to drink. We walked and talked and rested and before night we came to Nazareth, tired and hungry. Our lodgings were arranged by the women again and paid for, and we kept the same room as Jesus after our meal, but he ate and spoke little. Did he have foreboding about his visit? We sat together, men and women, and Jesus spoke to us about Nazareth; we asked if he would visit his family. He said again his family followed him everywhere, almost as if he had no personal family at all, in that everyone, or no one, was his family.

We were puzzled by this mix of statements and wondered what his family thought of him. Were they with the Pharisees or did they listen to his words with open hearts? Could they accept that their own son and brother was the Messiah? We were soon to find out the next day when he went to read in the synagogue. We followed him there and sat and listened to this reciting. Those inside and out were somber. During his first visit he was invited to read from Isaiah, but now he chose his own verse. He read in Hebrew.

I heard it said behind me, "This is Jesus who betrayed us last time he was here, saying we were not worthy of him, and he declared himself the anointed of Elijah, the Messiah." And they took the previous condemnation seriously. They remembered how they tried to drive him off a cliff, but he escaped and now he had returned to taunt them. So, they resented him, and refused to listen a second time.

Someone called out, "Where does he get his powers from?," and another, "This is Jesus, the carpenter, the son of Mary. What does he know?"— the same as they did the first visit only more vociferously. Then they listed his brothers and sister and asked if he would greet them. Remarkably, Jesus responded to them with: "A prophet is not without honor, except in his hometown, and in his own family."

We took that to mean that his family also thought him distracted, and not the Messiah. Then he said that even Elijah was rejected and his blessings fell on outsiders, and Nazareth would be put aside from his favors.

He was then told that his mother and family awaited him, but he did not go to them. He thought it better to avoid them and continued preaching, emphasizing the imminent coming of God, although the numbers were much fewer, and he even found it difficult to cure those who came to him, for the place abounded in disbelief. There seemed to be, strangely, some dwindling of his power. Jesus was visibly upset and left the synagogue to take refuge because the anger and skepticism of the people were growing, and he said again that Nazareth would not experience his releasing power, and it became unsafe to remain.

We hid him for the night and, as I was walking with Andrew on the streets, I heard it said that the prophet had to be killed; he was a sinner and a blasphemer. We returned and told the others. Simon the Zealot said we must spirit him away that night. I disagreed, saying he needed to rest but we would escape the next day. And so, in the early still of the morning we sneakily, like thieves, left Nazareth and made our way to Galilee, which took us four days, and the people on the way were mostly warm and greeted us with food and water and hospitality.

Once there, Jesus gathered his disciples together and sat them down and told them it was time to go among the people and tell them what they have seen and heard. He said to spread the good news that God's kingdom is at hand, to tell them to repent and to love one another as he had taught us. He would send us twelve first and later many other disciples into the world to proclaim his message, and he would send us out two by two, and I would walk with Andrew.

We were hesitant. We knew this was coming; but were we ready? Jesus dismissed our concerns saying we were full of the spirit and anyone who was not entirely convinced must leave now because they could not endure what was to come. He warned us many would listen and hear, but many would curse us. But those towns that did not welcome us would not be honored and we were to leave the town by dusting our shoes of its dirt, and those towns that rejected us will be treated like Sodom and Gomorrah. "Stay in the same house that accepts you, take nothing you need but rely on the people to support you. Those who are of the spirit will give in spirit."

We looked at each other and Jesus promised us we would have the gift of healing and casting out of demons. We didn't want to leave him. But he said he would stay in Galilee and preach the word, for the word was to be spread by many as he could not reach everyone needing to be released from sin, and the multitudes could not be save individually, but they must individually experience the word of God and respond. When he told us we would meet again we were pacified and set out with John and James in the direction of the Dio. I asked Andrew if he was confident, and he said he had seen and heard enough to be convinced. Others went in different directions.

So, we went on to various towns, and at first, I was uncomfortable and had no voice, and few people gathered to listen. But as soon as we started casting out demons their interest grew, and soon, we had small crowds listening and questioning. I taught them as I had been taught by Jesus, to repent and prepare for God's coming. I was amazed at my ability to dispel demons and cure the sick simply by laying on my hands. I told them it was not my power but through another that I could do these things. I told them of the Messiah and that his message was from God, and we were to heed it at once, and fully. If they did not respond then they would be discarded at the judgment. We preached eternal life and more people came to hear, for it was initially intriguing and appealing in light of their customs and traditions. They didn't dismiss us as I thought, but considered our words, especially that the coming of the kingdom of God was imminent, and the only way to prepare was to repent.

They asked, "What is this kingdom?"

I answered that it was the new heaven where sin and suffering would vanish and everlasting peace would reign on all men. This they took exception to. "All men? But how? Only Jews know their God and their God knows them." They also said it is taught that when men die, they vanish.

"Are the Romans to worship our God?" they asked. "The Romans have their own gods but they allow us our God. But they will accept the God of the Jews?"

"When the truth is revealed, there will be only one God," I answered.

"Who is our God? Who is this Jesus?"

"The Lord is our God," I spoke. "Jesus is the Son of Man, the Messiah."

They continued to protest. "There have been many sons of man, even sons of God; the emperor declares himself divine."

"But by their works you will know them," I replied.

I said that it is truly stated, but when the kingdom comes it will settle for all men and be for all men, but salvation will still come from the Jews, and shared with all men bowing to the one true God. But I told them those Jews who do not listen and do not repent and refuse the message and warnings will not be saved, but others will be saved in their place.

They were taken aback at this and turned away, but some remained. "Are we to make sacrifice every day to repent?" they asked.

I answered, "Yes, make sacrifice as it is ordained. But repentance, just like sin, is centered in the heart. Here a person must be cleansed and be honest and requite."

Then they asked, "Is all sin equally evil?"

I knew the Jewish law insofar as not all sins were considered equal, and there were many different ways to sin and many used false reasoning to acquit themselves. "All sins against God and man are evil, and the habit of sin is the prison of the heart. But man's law is not God's law."

"What is man's law if it is not the Scriptures? Moses gave us the law."

"The law is to love all," I replied. "That is God's law."

"We know the law," they continued. "A sin against man also is a sin against God because God gave us the law."

I said that any act that defiles or hurts another, whether it be gossip, lying, or insults were also sins against God. Jesus teaches us the law of love and breaking that law is breaking God's law.

"What is this law of love?" they asked.

"Love everyone as if they are family and there you will find comfort. For sin against another is sickness of the heart. It is stated in the Scriptures that you shall love your neighbor as yourself."

"What's the punishment for sin?" they asked.

"Death," I replied.

"All men die," they said.

I said that any act that defiles or hurts another were also sins against God. Jesus teaches us the law of love and breaking that law is breaking God's law. Those who kept this law would never die.

"And repentance? What is it you speak of?"

I replied, "Sorrow for sins. True remorse. Reparation."

"How do we know when we are truly remorseful? Do we wear sackcloth and ashes as it is stated?'

"Yes," I said, "but you must not sin again. You must turn away from sin sincerely."

With that they felt helpless because they knew the weakness of their nature. "What of minor sins? Why are they important? Can we be damned for lesser sins?"

I told them minor sins were dangerous because they were cracks in the building and cracks will widen if unattended until the building has fallen. Also, our natures are God-given and must be good, hence our sins are our doing, because we see value in things where there is none; we see advantage and satisfaction where there is only deception.

And as they listened and looked up to me, I felt enabled. I was indeed attracting men and women by the word and each word I spoke revealed a truth more striking. And I was replete as I had never felt before, except when Jesus had called me. Now I knew my destiny and my duty and I had denied the trivial things I thought important once, and acceptance of the divine message. Nothing mattered anymore—not my family, my boat, my business, my house—stronger at every word, and more precise, as I taught and understood clearly what had been uncertain before.

And Andrew was with me and we both preached the kingdom of God and learnt from each other, and cured the sick. And for some months we continued until one day we heard of the execution of the baptizer. It was said it was Herod's new wife, Herodias, who wanted the accuser dead, and Herod acquiesced. But it was certain that he also feared the people, and had considered John a growing problem for his authority.

After the death of John, Andrew was inconsolable for many days. I thought John a good man and a worthy one but I did not know if he was a prophet. But this man led many into righteousness and favor, and he had anointed Jesus as his successor. It was also said that Herod had heard of Jesus and was disturbed by the reports. This was even more worrying. Herod said Jesus was John the baptist reincarnated, and his growing obsession with Jesus was a sign of future malady.

8

THE BREAD OF LIFE

SURE ENOUGH, ALL THE DISCIPLES returned to Capernaum in time and we embraced our Master and there was sorrow and pain. For the baptist had been the light and he was much loved, and Jesus said John was the last of the prophets of the Lord. But we had many good things to tell him as everyone had been busy spreading the word and had experienced moments of elation and disappointment, but, overall, they were proud and happy to be messengers. And they spoke how they healed, and people followed them and questioned them. And the words came into their mouths and everything that he had said sat easily on their minds and came effortlessly, for they had been well instructed, and many believed and were baptized.

Then Jesus told us he was pleased, and that we had worked hard and should rest a while, and so we took another boat on the sea and headed north as he wanted to be away from the crowds, as he suffered most from the death of John. But to our surprise when we arrived at the bank of Bethsaida there were more crowds waiting for him. He went to them and healed and spoke to them and their enthusiasm grew, and he preached to them.

Andrew was amazed at the size of the crowd and he said there must be thousands. Matthew said about five thousand. When Jesus spoke, they were deathly quiet, so his voice hovered above the lapping of the water and the birds and the breeze. Again, those in the front sometimes repeated his words to those behind, and they sat still and listened eagerly, for words of his miracles preceded him. Many came so they could believe, many were curious and some lighthearted, but all stayed until dusk, when I told Jesus that they should be dispersed so they could go to the town to take their meal.

Jesus, however, was so impressed with the multitude that he felt pity and said they must not be turned away hungry. I remember he asked Philip where he could buy bread; Philip replied they did not have enough money, and they carried only five loaves and two fish. Jesus said to bring them to him and he prayed over them and said to distribute the food amongst the people. As we did so, there was more food available. It was astonishing that at the end of the meal we collected twelve baskets full of leftovers.

The people proclaimed him their king and their enthusiasm was overwhelming. Everything that he had taught them that day was fortified by that miracle. Never had the crowds been so accepting.

Again, Jesus said that it was natural that God provided for his people, as natural as sown seeds produce greater amounts than their number. After the crowds had dispersed Jesus told us to sail towards Capernaum, while he would go alone to the mountain to pray and rest, and meet up later.

That night, the sea was rolling again in the wind, and we struggled to make headway and rested when we could and took turns on watch. Later in the evening, Simon the Zealot was on watch and saw something in the distance, not far from the shore. It was the figure of a man. Simon woke us and he shouted that someone was standing on the water.

We all looked. There was occasional moonlight between the clouds and the reflection on the water and movement of the waves made it hard to see properly. "He's standing on the shore," Thomas said. Then John said he was in the sea on a sandbank and wanted help. I was convinced the man was standing on the water, and we were afraid it was a ghost. But then the man shouted out to us not to be afraid: it was he, Jesus.

I immediately wanted to jump in and help him but instead I said, "Lord, call me, and I will come to you on the water." As we neared, he asked me to come and help him into the boat, and before I got out of the boat I momentarily looked into the deep water, and the waves were rising, and pain struck my legs as I entered the water, and as I sank Jesus put out his hand and held me and we stood on solid water, and we returned to the boat with the help of the others.

When the storm had ceased, we were on the west bank. And there were people waiting there, for many had heard about the loaves and fishes and came wanting to greet him. They walked by the boat and Jesus stood near them and said they had followed him not because of the signs he had given them but because he had filled their bellies. They were reproached and fell silent. Jesus continued that the food they ate was momentary satisfaction, but in time all food would spoil, except that the bread which he offered them would last eternally.

They asked, "Where is such food?"

He replied, "It is the spiritual food of God. The manna that God sent to Moses and his people was eaten and they died, but whoever eats of the bread of heaven will never die."

They were affronted and unsure how to respond. This bread of eternal life of which he spoke fascinated but mystified them. Who did not want to live forever? And Jesus stunned them by saying he was the bread of life, and whoever ate his flesh and drank his blood would never die.

This caused consternation and the old argument resurfaced that he was only Jesus, son of Mary and Joseph; how could he talk like this? How can he say he has come down from heaven? They were annoyed and argued amongst themselves. Eat his flesh? Just like the pagans?

Jesus tried to put a wedge between the spirit and the body but they were disturbed and faltered at the mention of the spirit, for they were not used to hearing it. He said the body counted for nothing; the spirit gives life. "How can the body die yet the spirit live?" they asked; he spoke of things not real to them.

They were disappointed, and started to drift away. The body counts for nothing? How could they accept this? "God gave us our body. We must live with our body and work and give praise and sacrifice, and eat and celebrate, and we will reunite after death, but it counts for nothing?"

Jesus turned to us and said no one comes to him except those whom the Father has sent, and none will be lost who are sent. Then he ruefully asked us if we wanted to leave too. I said to him, "Master, where are we to go? You are the way to eternal life."

Jesus then set his eyes on a mountain in the distance and said, "I have done so many miraculous things, but still, they do not live in the spirit, only by what they can eat and drink and wear and buy in the market. They care for their own family, but not the children of God. These cities, Capernaum, Chorazin, Bethsaida, I have given my all and still they will not repent and heed the Spirit. They will be cursed because even the pagans and gentiles would bow down in repentance if they witnessed what these cities have seen and heard. And it will not go well for them—they who reject the Lord, are themselves rejected."

He was distraught because so many left but none that his Father had sent him.

That evening when Jesus had been taken away by the women to his lodgings, we entered a boardinghouse paid from the collection purse Judas Iscariot carried, and all gathered in the main room. The owner was a disciple and boarded upstairs, and we sat and ruminated on the day.

We were quiet with our thoughts until Bartholomew spoke up. "I heard Herod is looking for Jesus. The crowds are too great—much larger than the baptist's—and he is worried."

John then said, "Yes, they will take him away one day. But so far, they have left him alone. The Romans are not as concerned, but they listen to the Herodians."

"It's becoming more dangerous every day," I replied.

"Are you worried?" asked Philip.

I said, "Jesus speaks freely and is not concerned about it. He attacks the Pharisees, the priesthood, and the Sadducees and the scribes for their hypocrisy, but not everyone who listens is in agreement."

Then Philip spoke again, "Do you really believe Jesus is from God?"

I said, "Yes. His message is contrary to what we expected, and the things he speaks of are new to us. He says those who hear and believe are his disciples, but many take home his words and think on them. But he sees that as being light. He needs immediate absolute conviction on first hearing to accomplish his mission because the time is now. If the words touch you, you're alive and you must respond, as we have, my brothers and sisters, for the kingdom is at hand. And for most people the truth of his words is hindered by everyday chores and necessities and the Pharisees and their duties which must be put aside."

But Philip protested that we debated every night—was that being light? And I said, "We are fortunate to have that luxury while we are with him, to discuss amongst ourselves the things he says and does, to fortify our commitment which is already given, to listen to what people are saying, but when the time comes, we must be solid and unwavering."

Andrew agreed. "The coming is imminent, as Jesus said, and the people don't have the time for debate, or they would end up like the Pharisees themselves. We must heed the message and live as if tomorrow the Lord God will come as prophesized."

But Thomas was resistant. He said Jesus' words about his flesh and blood were not easy. Judas Iscariot and Simon agreed, saying many turned away when they had heard this. It was not from Moses, and it was against the law to drink blood. It was from the Greek pagans to eat a god's flesh in order to live like the god. Jesus should explain more so that people would not wonder so much. I replied that his words were the bread and water of eternal life, that they will replenish the spirit in this deceitful world. Heeding the word, even if puzzling, was the same as spiritual nourishment.

James asked, "Do you think it means we really must eat his body and drink his blood?"

I said I was not sure but bread is bread and not flesh. Wine was wine. If he changes them into his flesh and blood it is done miraculously as the bread is still bread and the wine still wine, as we saw. But in the world of the Spirit, anything was possible for him, because he was of the Spirit of God, and the Spirit was in him. If the bread is his body, let it be so; the truth cannot be contradicted.

With that we slept but I wanted to hear from Mary, and Joanna and Salome and Susanna, what they thought in the morning, because I knew they were personally inspired.

We set out for Galilee again in the morning and as we were preparing, I saw Judas Iscariot pocket some money from the collection bag. I let it pass and as soon as I could I told the Master and he was not surprised. "How much did he take?"

I told him a handful of coins. "Good, we still have enough for the nights' lodgings and meals then. If you confront him, he will deny it; don't make his burden even heavier."

After that time Jesus took us to places previously not visited and avoided the places he had cursed. I don't remember him going to Chorazin but others said he had, but then he extended his missionary area far outside the regular circle. This included such places as Genezareth, Tyra, and Sidon, then south and eastward and the northern part of Decapolis and Caesarea Philippi.

In Genezareth he was confronted by the Pharisees, some of whom were following as usual. It seemed a trivial comment when they chided Jesus for allowing us, his disciples, to eat without washing our hands. But Jesus took up the point and drew much angst from it, in terms I still do not agree with, entirely. He told them what goes into a man's mouth does not make him unclean, which we took to be a denial of our food laws. He went on to say that what comes out of a man's mouth makes him unclean.

We understood because he had spoken before that lying and slander and gossip and blasphemy show a man as unclean, but still, we were puzzled about the food restrictions which we always observed. The washing of hands was not significant since not all of Jews practiced it anyway. But Jesus' rebuke broke into the inner core of the Pharisees' authority. For the tradition designed and imposed by the Pharisees made it binding on everyone, even though the laws were originally ascribed to the high priests only.

Jesus said the Pharisees, those upholders of the tradition, would break the law or find loopholes declaring tradition equal to the law, and be self-justifying. Jesus then again declared the Pharisees hypocrites because they said one thing and did another; their hearts were evil even though they presented as righteous.

His meaning was clear when it came to what makes a man unclean: it is his profane language that defiles him, and the thoughts and intentions of lust, murder, slander, and lying originate in the heart and emerge through the mouth. That much was clear. But the food restrictions were not important?

That night I was alone with Joanna as she had followed us on that journey and we were accommodated together as it sometimes happened with wives of the disciples. I asked her if she agreed with Jesus about the food laws? She agreed. She had always found the Pharisaic traditions a burden and Jesus lightened the load by putting emphasis on the Commandments of God and the law of Moses.

But more importantly he distinguished between outward observance and the inner ordinance. If they were not in unison, then rightly we were condemned as hypocrites. Only God could see into a man's heart, but when a man spoke or acted, what was inside would eventually come out for all to see.

She said finally that he had said before that he had come to fulfill the law, not to replace it. I said I knew it but so much of what he said seemed to oppose the law. She said no, he shows us the law in a new light, as it should be taught and understood and practiced. He emphasized certain aspects over others and revealed the inner self as the true upholder of righteousness, strength, and divine approval. Hence, sinners we once regarded as unclean may in fact be clean inside, and the washed observers of the law, unclean. True cleanliness comes from the pure, selfless intention.

Again, she explained to me clearly what I had missed and as she spoke, I admired her even more. It was something not encountered before, and even though we knew the Lord God looks at the heart, we had forgotten. It was dawning on me that the inner self was flexible and reverted from honesty to deceit and must be in constant adjustment. What we appeared to be may not be who we truly were, and what we see may not be truly what it is.

She had opened my eyes. As it was once spoken: "I will know all the prophets when in heaven, but will I recognize myself?"

We lay close together that night—silent and peaceful.

9

THE DECLARATION

IN THE MORNING JESUS AGAIN rose early and we set out for Tyra and Sidon. Over the next few weeks, we traveled far together and always Jesus showed the curious and willing the signs of the coming kingdom and told them to prepare, for the time was short. And many accepted and others turned away, as he said it would happen.

In one town there came a woman crying and beseeching Jesus to cure her daughter. She was, we heard, a Syrophoenician and a Canaanite, and hence, in our eyes, an opponent. And Jesus knew her to be a convert to Judea, and so not fully Jewish. But still she came and cried even though he told her directly that he had come to save Israel and its children, and that outsiders were not to be fed. But then she said something remarkable: "Even dogs eat the crumbs that fall from their master's table." Jesus was so impressed by this reply that he immediately cured her daughter.

But we knew that he was not intolerant of Syrians since he cured many, but he would not waste time on those who were half-hearted converts or those who were not of the God of Israel. This woman showed faith as a God-fearer, as many did, and Jesus told her so.

It was in Decapolis that Jesus again did something remarkable. We had traveled far to the north, east, and then southeast to northern Decapolis, then to the eastern part of Galilee, where he continued preaching and healing, and we listened carefully to every word for our own future mission. Amazingly, after feeding four thousand listeners with as little as seven loaves and a few fish as he had done before, the Pharisees and Sadducees combined, even though they were opposed to each other in many ways, to ask Jesus for a sign from heaven.

Of all the miracles he had done, including the present one, and witnessed by them, they still were not satisfied. They said they had seen miracle workers before and magicians, and they had their own exorcists and healers, and had even put others to death who were considered profane, but they wanted an unambiguous sign that Jesus was from God.

But Jesus turned to us and said that even then, would they believe? If the skies opened and God called out to them and struck them down, they would say it was a trick or an illusion—that the voice was lifted and the skies were controlled for the sake of making them look foolish, and the lightning produced by magic.

Jesus said to them that only one sign will be given: that of Jonas the prophet who spent three days underground—leaving them puzzled and argumentative.

When in the boat again to cross the sea, he warned us about the leaven of the Pharisees. For their words turned people from the truth. They demanded observation of the law but they were not observing it. He was adamant that the Pharisees were unfit for the kingdom and always railed against them, and they refused to believe him as they were proud and stubborn, except for a few. He accused them of making excuses for their laxity, but they were hard on the people. I asked him if he favored the Sadducees? And he answered they were more removed from the people and only cared about themselves.

But the Pharisees insisted to his listeners that they were the bearers of the law, not Jesus. Their authority was attested to by tradition; they were, with the scribes, interpreters of the law as ordained by the prophets, whereas Jesus was from the tribe of the false prophets and preachers and miracle workers, zealots and antagonists, who endangered the faith and the lives of the Judeans.

However, although they were set against him, and he against them, they never interfered with his mission. There were, as we knew, plots to stop him, but they never came to fruition. Perhaps in their hearts they knew something, or perhaps the time wasn't right, but they held to their authority throughout, while denying that of Jesus, and they let him preach and tried to get him to contradict himself, or exhibit ignorance or blasphemy, rather than resort to force.

Even the Romans and Herodians who were concerned about the size of his crowds waited, and saw the man as mad, perhaps. In short, outside of Jerusalem, Jesus was in no danger from the Pharisees or Romans, and they let him preach freely except when the Pharisees warned the people they were being led astray.

I told my fellow apostles, the twelve, that we were safe as long as we stayed away from Jerusalem. For there stood the cauldron of seething and discontent that made it unsafe for Jesus, as well as for ourselves—all temptations swirled inside its gates, and any incident could erupt and lead to an upheaval and Roman intervention. So, we were to continue as before.

From Bethsaida we entered Caesarea Philippi where Jesus cured a blind man, and we also did work in his name, curing and preaching. Many came to the disciples and we, like others, healed in his name, but some we could not heal.

Jesus then took us to a secluded place away from the crowds where water gushed from under a cliff surrounded by greenery and the sound was refreshing and renewing, and the undergrowth was in stark contrast to the stone and sand of the desert. He sat us there and we were absorbed in the moment as we rested and drank the water and reclined on the grass.

There was a town and a Roman temple not far away, but this section was private. Jesus spoke a little and was obviously distracted by something, and I wanted to discuss why some demons could not be expelled by us. He looked a little irritated and puzzled even, as if for one time, he was unsure of himself, or us.

He stood and motioned for us to remain seated until he asked, "Who do they say I am?"

John asked, "Who? The Pharisees? The multitudes? The disciples and followers?"

Philip answered, "Some say you are John the baptist reincarnated."

He said, "I have heard it."

"And others you are Elijah," replied Matthew, "or one of the prophets, some even say a demon."

"I have heard that, also." He kept walking in a circle, and then when he came close to me but seeming to address everyone, he asked, "But who do you say I am?"

I answered immediately for them, "We have seen and heard enough to know you are the Christ. We have been with you many months and witnessed your power and heard your teaching that only the Son of the everlasting God could produce."

The disciples agreed and turned to each other and murmured approval. At last, we had come to the point where there had to be no doubt that Jesus was the Messiah, and we were given wholeheartedly in our love and acceptance, and everyone was motivated by their own revelation. Jesus then looked pleased.

He stood me up and looked into my eyes with an immortal depth and acknowledged my conviction and told me my knowledge was from the Father, and I was the rock of his community, and will be called Peter, and all would depend on me, for what was lost or gained here, so it would be in heaven.

But I protested that Jesus himself was the foundation, but he said he would not always be with us and that we had all been chosen for a reason. He said he must go to Jerusalem to fulfill the word and the promise of salvation, and that he would be handed over to the authorities for persecution.

I protested again that this surely would not happen as long as we were with him. But he became vexed and said I did not understand what needed to be accomplished, and I saw things only as a prisoner sees his walls. He admonished me and said, "Get behind me Satan, you are my stumbling block. Do I tell you these things in jest? As one confined to this world?"

He said one must not fear for their life, as the coming of the kingdom brings new life and redemption. "If you try to preserve your life and what you have, you will surely lose it, but to lose your life in the name of the Son, you will reap your reward."

Sometimes I could see the vision of the new kingdom clearly; other times I was hindered by confusion.

Jesus then said as we left the water that we were not to tell anyone who he was and what had been revealed. On the way back Jesus exorcised a deaf mute which previously we could not. I asked him again why we did not have the power. He answered it was because we had not the faith of a mustard seed, and with only that much faith we could move mountains or quell storms or bring the dead to life. Again, I thought I had faith, but I was proved wrong. How could it be so elusive? What did it take to believe in him and myself without any doubt whatsoever? That is, to live in the state of utter conviction?

That night we stayed in the town and met some of the women who gave us lodgings, and I said to John that Jesus was adamant that he would go to Jerusalem, but it was a mistake. We had to dissuade him. John simply said who were we to question him? He then said Jesus had singled me out as the leader and the successor. Why did I still question what needed to be done? He said Jesus himself knew of the dangers there but there was something driving him on, and we must support him, as we always did.

I suspected some of the disciples questioned why I was chosen to be leader. From that day I was called Simon Peter, or just Peter. Jesus had already given me the name Cephas, which had the same meaning. I know they talked amongst themselves but I did not deserve the privilege, as I had many failings and could not imagine why I had been selected, or in fact, if I had been, but that was how it was taken.

What was this new community he spoke about? Were we to remain Jews or become something else? Did I have the strength to fulfill what he had started? Were we to convert the whole of Judea to his new teachings, almost like to a new religion? It was such an enormous undertaking for a few simple men from Galilee, to remove the people from their apathy and entrenched beliefs. The instability caused by such actions could be disastrous.

Whether the other disciples coalesced behind me or not was evidenced by their discussion which was to follow in the weeks ahead. But they said nothing to me then.

10

Transformations

IN THE MORNING, WE SET out to the north towards Capernaum when, after about a week on the road, Jesus rested one afternoon after preaching and took James, John, and myself aside and told the others not to follow. We went with him; he said nothing then, and we climbed up to the top of a mountain. Our hands and feet were scratched and the slope was steep and difficult, but he continued upwards until he was satisfied and the mountain flattened out and we were able to rest.

He told us to wait a while and stood on the top of a rock and raised his arms. He told us not to be afraid, but to be witnesses. At first there was nothing but then gradually like the dawn a majestic light shone from the sky and illuminated him. His face changed and he looked much younger, placid, almost like a boy again. And there was a high-sounding whirring like the wind at fever pitch on the mountain, and the clouds crossed the sun. His eyes were closed and we heard what sounded to be an unearthly voice amid the elements but I could not distinguish the words. And there were other figures forming in the clouds, and as they merged and swirled, pierced by sunlight, took on seemingly recognizable forms.

We covered our faces but Jesus came over to us and told us again not to fear, and there was, suddenly, nothing—and what we had seen, he said, must remain a secret, because no one would believe us and would only bring ridicule. We asked if the figures were of Moses and Elijah, and he said they were.

With this experience, we needed no more convincing. Jesus was the Son of God, who was our Father, and he had the approval of the prophets and the law. His majesty had been proven and we were in greater awe of him than ever. And on the basis of this metamorphosis, of both of Jesus and ourselves, we were to proclaim his glory and the coming of the Lord to all peoples.

But before we reached Capernaum, he told us all again that he would be betrayed into the hands of the authorities who will try to destroy him and eradicate him and all he taught. He even said he would be killed, but would be raised up after three days, and we did not question him, as we were reluctant to oppose him. But we looked to each other in a type of bafflement but remained repressed and spoke little, for the meaning was not clear.

Raised up? Then he would be killed but would not die? He referred to himself as the Son of Man, which we took to mean "Messiah," and his accusers would be the scribes and chief priests, and his death would be at the hands of the gentiles, who we understood to be the Romans?

After the event on the mountain, this was hard to accept, and we put it aside as something daunting, perhaps futuristic and beyond comprehension.

In Capernaum many came out to greet him and the women again came to him in numbers, and I met Joanna and Mary, and they welcomed us. Joanna took me home and we sat and talked and I told her I believed that Jesus was the Son of God. She seemed pleased with that as if she already knew, and we had tea, and I could only think of the inhuman voice or trembling above the mountain like an unearthly echo—was it the thunder in the clouds? Did we all hear the same thing? John said he heard the voice distinctly.

I told her Jesus was human, but not of this world. She said she knew, and we repeated some of his sayings which were like breaths of air. A new knowledge and identity were before us, a new truth, and the old ways must be accommodating, but to what extent? We agreed that if Jesus had not come to abolish the law, then he must have come to open our eyes and live as we must, together, in order to receive the Lord in a new spirit, and prepare to live in the New kingdom.

Jesus said that before we die, we would see him come and the world would be transformed, as predicted by the prophets. Joanna said we could not rest, and we had to spread the news, as none could be left out. And then I told her that he said he would be killed in Jerusalem and would be raised after three days, and she wept. But then she smiled through her tears, which

I dried, and I kissed her eyes and brushed her hair back. She said, "You are a good man, Simon."

I then told her that he had given me the name of Peter, and the authority to direct the disciples and lead the apostles. But what did I know of such things?

Then, she said, "You know what you must do, and I will not hamper you, Peter. You are the first among them and must spread the faith, as he has taught you."

In the morning, we met Jesus and there was a fuss about paying taxes in the town. I was asked by the tax gatherer if Jesus paid his taxes and I said he did. He then wanted me to pay my taxes even though we were exempt, being from the city. Jesus however asked me to catch a fish that he pointed out, near the surface, and to find a silver coin in its mouth. This I did and, sure enough, I found the coin that it had taken, and paid the taxes. Had Jesus seen the coin fall into the water, as there was much trading on the wharf?

"Better to pay than cause trouble," he said, and walked away. But the other disciples were surprised that Jesus should pay my taxes and started to question if in heaven, I, Peter, would be above the rest.

I was angry at the question since I never thought of myself as greater than any other but we all, it must be admitted, thought that our powers that Jesus had given us were something special. He had chosen us to spread the word and pay him homage. He entrusted us with a great task and we couldn't help but think a little highly of ourselves. Questions were asked if James, John, and myself were somehow more favored, and how it would be in heaven?

Jesus came back, having heard some of the talk, and he took us to some shade where there were seats and refreshments which the women provided. Children were playing around us and Jesus said unless we become like little children we cannot enter heaven. Some of the disciples had children and wondered what he meant, for children, they knew, were reckless and disobedient, and needed discipline.

He said children were humble and did not prize any status. Ranking was something that men did once exposed to the world. Men put themselves into an order according to the worldly values, but in heaven, as with all things, status was reversed—the humblest were considered the mightiest. And he warned against false humility which is obvious when one performs good deeds for the poor in public. He told us again to give alms in private, pray in private, do penance in private, so no one knows you did them, although it was contrary to custom.

Then the mother of the sons of Zebedee came and asked Jesus if her sons James and John could sit at his right and left hand in heaven. He scoffed a little and said she did not know what she was asking, for the ordeal was greater than men could bear.

He then turned and said if the children of God will fall, woe to the man who makes them fall; it would be better for him to be drowned with a millstone, which was an astonishing thing to say. Was he advocating suicide, which was considered the most abominable of crimes? Or severe punishment outside of the law? What did he mean?

And we are all children of the Father, he continued, so he protects his own, and will rejoice when one who is lost through sin is found again, for he has not been sent to save the righteous, but the sinner.

Jesus could not possibly have meant what he said. But it brought home to us the seriousness of sin, and its inevitability, which was a chasm no man could climb out from alone. He admitted men would sin, but without repentance and forgiveness, they were doomed.

He then elaborated on how we should deal with another who transgresses us. We should settle disputes amicably, within the community. If one's brother refuses to listen or be agreeable, cast him out. I then asked Jesus how many times we should forgive another. He answered as many times as he asks for forgiveness, if contrition is really from the heart. But the man who asks for forgiveness in deceit or false pleading will not be forgiven. And what mercy is shown to you, you must show to others.

After these conversations and warnings, we retreated to our lodgings, but not before some of his followers invited him to go with them to attend the Feast of the Tabernacles in Jerusalem. I was certain he should not go there. And he declined, even though he said before he was heading for Jerusalem. He said he was not ready to go there. But he told them they should go without him.

I I

THE FEAST OF THE TABERNACLE

JESUS WAS REFORMING THE WAY we lived and how we treated each other in preparation for the kingdom. He was forging a new community with a new relationship with God, not a new God. Already the priority of love was germinating in the community, but could it last? Could we always be so stringent with our actions and thoughts? So brotherly and sisterly? Jesus said the kingdom was imminent; perhaps our desire for perfection would only need to last until then, and then it would be easier when love pervaded all and everything around us.

We went to Jesus in the morning and he was with Mary talking as we gathered. They sent on three disciples with money to a town in Samaria where we would spend the night. Jesus well knew the enmity between Jews and the Samaritans. It was a long, spiteful feud, but he was so confident in his lack of animosity that he thought he would be duly accepted. And news of the meeting with the Samaritan woman at the well was already legend.

Then, after first refusing to accompany his disciples, he said he was going on to Jerusalem. I asked him why he wanted to go to there as it was dangerous given the opposition of the Pharisees and Sadducees, as well as the zealots. He did not answer directly except to say that the Scriptures had to be fulfilled, and that would happen in good time, but he seemed reluctant to go, and would travel to Samaria first.

We set out the next day and advanced through some peaceful countryside. As we expected, the few he had sent returned from the Samaritan town and said he would not be accepted because they assumed he was going to Jerusalem, which the Samaritans detested. The Samaritans long believed that they could worship outside of Jerusalem, on their sacred Mount Gerizim, but this was denied by the Jews—worship was to be in Jerusalem only. The townspeople refused him accommodation. John and James were furious and, known as Sons of Thunder, asked permission to have the place destroyed.

Jesus said the answer was not violence; hostility cannot be met with hostility, and they had not come after him violently with swords, and because he understood their position, he moved on to the next town where he was accepted for the night, as was customary.

The next day he followed the road to the east of the Jordan, and as we walked we attracted attention, and many greeted us and waved and called out; some were dumb in their defiance or rejection, some curious and walked along a little way when one man we believed to be a scribe from the cloak he wore said to Jesus, "Wait, and I will follow you everywhere." But Jesus did not wait. "Where shall the Son of Man put his head? Even the wild animals have shelter for rest." We took this to mean that Jesus did not ignore the scribe, but that he was really telling him of the terrible hardships ahead if indeed he followed, and he would fall behind for he would face unbearable trials.

Jesus was then impressed with another man who stood before him, and Jesus accepted him and said to follow him, but the man had to attend his father's funeral, and he would follow later. Jesus said, "Which is more important, the dead or the coming of the kingdom?" He also left him behind. And then a third and last said, "I will follow you but I will say good-bye to my wife first." To which Jesus replied, "There can be no looking back once you have decided to walk with me." And again, the would-be disciple was left on the side of the road.

As we went on, Jesus came to rest, and as we sat in the shade he looked at us and could see we were surprised at his rejection of the would-be disciples. "Believe me, nothing is more important than my work. There can be no doubt that the work I do is more important than family, or tradition, or ritual, or even your material life. But it is dangerous and hard but is above all else, even earthly relationships, for men are who they are, and I have told you before, he who finds his life shall lose it, and he who loses his life for my sake will find it."

Then later in the evening he gathered seventy of his followers and sent them out to preach two by two, as he had before, and to teach his message to every place, town, village, and city where he could not go. They were excited and went away optimistic, empowered with his authority.

We rested in our lodgings for the evening, Jesus with James and John, and I with Judas Iscariot and some others. Judas had been following constantly, and never questioned the Master. I was wondering about him. I had said nothing about the money I saw him take. But I think that he took no more, for we had abundance from donations and the wealthy who supported us.

We ate silently and I drank a little wine and ate some olives that had been left by the innkeeper. Judas did not drink. He just wanted to sleep but I asked him if he would be with Jesus to the end. He answered yes, but he said Jesus paid him little attention. He had not involved him in any discussion or recognized his abilities. I asked him if he had doubts. He said he was accepting of the miracles but there were too many, and the people expected this wherever we went now, and their impact was reducing the significance of his message.

I said, "Do you think he tricks people?"

He answered, "No, but you said he raised from the dead, you saw it, but can it be? Does any man deny God that right? Does he take the sanctity of death from individuals, calling back to life from their repose, to die again?"

I said it was within his power. But then he asked, "Why do so many people turn away? Why don't they all leave their ploughs and bakeries and hammers and follow him if he can raise from the dead? Why do so many think he is a charlatan or a blasphemer? Why do the religious teachers accuse him of being sent by Beelzebub?"

I told him because if everyone followed him there would be no need for him to be sent in the first place. Not all can be saved. And he said, "Then we must bury our doubts and cast all away and follow him because he says so?"

I was silent. I wanted to tell him about the metamorphosis I witnessed but I could not. I felt sorry for Judas; he did seem alone, but Jesus accepted him above the scribes and others on the road, so he must have known something. Judas even wondered why he was chosen. I had never seen him preaching to crowds but he did spread the word quietly along the way to small groups. And people listened to him and debated with him and they were attracted to him. But mainly he went along with us and kept his place, that was all.

Some days later we ventured to the lower part of Peraea and the seventy returned and told us of their deeds and how the people were accepting of their message and assurances and believed in the Lord without even seeing him. There was happiness and we celebrated that night, and in the morning headed to Jericho.

The road was meandering and scrubby and mainly desolate, but we were together in number and with Jesus, so we were not afraid, but the road was often used by robbers and had the name of the "Way of Blood" for its many violent robberies.

And just outside of Jericho a lawyer was waiting in readiness. He was with some others and must have heard of our coming and waited on the side of the road. When he saw Jesus, he came up to him, well presented as a lawyer, and addressed him as "Rabbi" and "Master," and said he had heard that Jesus was from God and had proclaimed eternal life. He therefore asked directly how one can achieve this life: "Tell me, so I can do it."

The lawyer valued his own life and wanted to ensure life everlasting since he was privileged and well satisfied. Because he was a lawyer Jesus used a legal device to have the accused convict himself. He asked, "What is written?" The man was taken aback as he assumed Jesus would give him his answer, not a question. The lawyer answered, "To love God and love your neighbor as yourself."

Jesus said he answered correctly, but the lawyer must have known that, and so he asked, perhaps out of curiosity but possibly to ensnare Jesus, who his neighbor was. That was something that was not written.

Jesus told a story about a man, possibly a Jew, who was attacked on the road and robbed and left for dead. Three men crossed his path—a priest, a Levite, and the Samaritan. Only the Samaritan helped him, generously taking him to an inn and paying the innkeeper.

Jesus asked, "Who was the attacked man's neighbor?"

The lawyer answered somewhat hesitantly, "The Samaritan, who showed him compassion?"

Jesus then said, "You know what to do, go and do it."

It was hard to accept because of the hatred of Samaritans, and their hatred towards us. But I knew he was saying in the kingdom of God mercy and unity shall reign, not hatred or division, and if one could not dissolve their enmity, they could not enter.

That night I was with Andrew and we thought about the parable, and wondered why Jesus told stories, as if the listeners were children, and did we agree with the Samaritan being our neighbor? Andrew said the hatred of Jew and Samaritan was so deep it could not be rectified. But I saw that perhaps the hatred was not the fault of individuals as it was inbred in a people as a culture. So, it was something one could overcome—one to one. Perhaps that was the secret. You couldn't love a race of people the same as you couldn't convert them, but the one next to you, the one in need and suffering, you could love, no matter who they were.

Andrew agreed and said also that the parables had many dimensions but they were not always obvious. Joanna was not with us as she had returned to Capernaum, but Mary was still traveling with us, and I wanted to ask her if Jesus spoke in parables, what was it that we might miss, as the meaning was not always clear.

But there was no opportunity as in the morning Jesus set out again for Jerusalem and entered Bethany first where a woman named Martha welcomed him into her house for a meal. While she was preparing, she complained about having to do all the work and that Mary, her sister, should help her. Mary sat at the feet of Jesus listening to him, and I and some others who were invited agreed with Martha.

Jesus, however, told Martha not to fuss because Mary was learning and was preoccupied, otherwise she would have helped. It was in keeping with the Lord's command to leave all and follow him, for in relation to what was at stake, no amount of inconsequential worry or work could replace the short time with him. Hence, we left family and friends and followed him, but someone had to do the work. So, I thought at the time, both had chosen well. But Mary's choice was more appropriate since Jesus would only stay a short time, and Martha was in no need of instruction.

We then went on to Jerusalem and arrived there for the feast. I remember it was hectic, almost chaotic with animals, food, dust, shouting, and general upheaval. Thousands were mingling and feasting and setting up their booths, but Jesus did so in private, at first.

The crowds were heavy and the mood excited and unsettled. There were those who asked where Jesus was and his name was mentioned, and some discussed if he was a true prophet. We heard these things as we wandered and ate, but kept silent. We also heard, as Jesus predicted, that there was angst felt towards him because he defied the Pharisees, and we went back but could not find him. In fact, for days we were without him and in that time, we heard that there was a Jewish plot to kill him.

The Feast of the Tabernacle

Near the end of the feast there was a hubbub coming from the temple, and we went there and found Jesus teaching and discussing. We feared for him, as many inside seemed aroused by the occasion and unusually restless. We went near and we heard the Pharisees ask each other how an ignorant man could be so learned, and on whose authority did he speak? Jesus said his authority was from God, which was obvious to those who did the will of God and kept the law of Moses.

Jesus spoke without fear and said that the people were cursed, because it was Moses who was their lawgiver and at the center of their self-identity as Jews, not the Pharisees. It was a vicious attack. The people asked why he was allowed to preach in the temple if he was so corrupt. Jesus then brazenly accused them of wanting to kill him. Many knew it was true but the Pharisees mocked him for being mad, and still his presence was tolerated. Some people asked why he shouldn't be thrown out. Or did the authorities secretly believe him and were afraid of him?

We listened but remained silent. But the sense that the Pharisees were in trouble with their own people was obvious. They had to keep face. And to make it worse, he criticized the people of Israel who did not know their own God, because they did not know the one who was sent by him, but he, Jesus, knew him.

I wanted to take him away then, quickly, as the mood was mounting, but some defended him, saying what more can a man do than he has done? We moved closer to him, about six of us, to show him we would protect him, and wanted him to leave, but he incited them even more. "If anyone is true to my word, they will have everlasting life." And they criticized him because Abraham and the prophets were all dead, and yet Jesus told them that Abraham saw this day come, and rejoiced.

Having said that they laughed at him. "How could you have seen Abraham? You're not even fifty years old!" And he said, mysteriously, to them, to arouse them even more: "Before Abraham was, I am." We then went to him and covered him and took him away as many took up stones and threw at him, cursing him.

We went back to the booth but the upheaval continued. Turning the people against him, the Pharisees looked to each other in satisfaction as their argument that he was possessed with a blasphemous demon took hold.

That night we slept in the tent, the twelve of us, but Jesus went outside and hid in secret so we would not be harmed. I turned to Andrew. "He is upset that the people reject him. Did he think that it would be easy to turn their heads?"

Andrew was silent but then said, "They are sure of who they are and they follow the Pharisees and the way of the world, for it is all they know and trust in."

I said, "He is more annoyed that they reject his Father, their own God, whom they say they worship, but do not really know."

Andrew agreed. "He must offend and humiliate and provoke to get people to see how they sin, the way they have strayed from the law and from God. They are too proud in their certainty that they are God's children, and that they will be delivered and live and die and live again as proclaimed. Jesus retracts that certainty, and they are left in confusion."

I said, "But did you hear his words, 'Before Abraham was, I am?' He spoke them softly, maybe all did not hear, but many did. Is he saying he is God?"

Andrew retreated, "No, emphatically, no. If, as you say, he is the Son of God, he is divine, he is from God, and of God, but not God. He always claims his power is from God. How could the people ever accept that he was God? It would remove every last one of his followers."

I said, "Then what does he mean? I heard the baptist say he has always lived, spiritually, perhaps in different forms or personages, perhaps as the Son of God." I thought and then said, "For the moment, we will abide. We will see what the future brings."

I knew we were excited when we worked miracles in his name and proclaimed the kingdom, but what if he left us? Would we continue with his mission or return to the sea? How would we proceed? Once he was gone, what would happen to us? Would the kingdom of God still come upon us?

Then, near the end of the feast, Jesus was seen again wandering with head covered, and we walked behind him, but some Pharisees recognized him and they did not berate him but asked him to go with them. He uncovered his head and followed them outside the temple where a small crowd had gathered. We followed behind.

A woman had been brought to the Pharisees on the charge of adultery. They said she was taken from the bed. "She should be stoned," the Pharisees said.

"It is the law," they said again.

"Then if it is the law, do it."

He then knelt on the dirt and drew with his finger. The Pharisees looked and were stunned, but still they insisted she should be stoned. He drew again in the dirt. I could not see what he drew. Then Jesus stood and said, "Be it so, then the one without sin should cast first."

The people, one by one, dropped their rocks and walked away. Jesus then looked at the woman with pity and asked her where were her accusers?

She said, "No one is left."

He said, "Then no one accuses you. Sin no more."

We turned to each other and wondered why he did not follow the law, since the woman was guilty of a grievous sin, and to pardon her was tantamount to compliance. But we dared not, and we held it in our thoughts, for she had not even asked for forgiveness. But the mercy he showed her explained his action.

Again, Jesus wandered amid the throngs until another crowd had gathered around him waiting to see more miracles. And he told them that soon they would not see him because he would go to the Father, whither they could not come, and he raised his voice and said that he was the water of life and they too could have this water if they believed. Further, he described himself as the light of the world, so that all could see and be saved from the perdition of sin.

The people were taken aback and many said he was the Messiah, but others scoffed and said that nothing good came out of Galilee and, anyway, how could he call others sinners when he sinned every day? The Pharisees, we were told, sent soldiers to arrest him then but they refrained because they too had never heard anything like this before, and they were afraid to lay hands on him as many still supported him.

We moved away from the crowd, but some still followed him. When we were fairly secluded, he said to us, "Likewise, you are the light of the world; you must show all your adherence to the law, forgiveness of sinners, and love of your neighbor. You will shine in honesty so that all may see. But I am the good shepherd, and not a hired hand. I know my sheep and they hear my voice. When one is lost, I put aside all to find him, and my sheep may come from a different flock, because they hear and come, and I know them. And for my sheep I will do anything. I will give my life to protect them, because it is my desire, not my paid duty."

Those remaining were pleased with his words and felt much comfort. "This is a true leader of men," they said, "a great prophet." Some followed us, but most went back to their booths and tents, unhappy that they could not change.

12

THE RESURRECTION AND THE LIFE

WE LEFT JERUSALEM AS IT was becoming too dangerous. We followed the road and on the Mount of Olives Jesus taught us a prayer. He said God already knew what we needed, so give thanks for what we had, and as I remember it, he said, "Dear Father in heaven, we honor you, we look forward to your kingdom, and follow your will; grant us our bread each day, and protect us from sin, and bring us to eternal life." But others may remember the words exactly. It was nothing like the prayers we recited every day, over and over, in accordance with the tradition.

It was a simple but moving prayer. We had been taught never to be so personal or direct with God and to follow the liturgy given to us for generations as formulaic and set in the language God could hear, in solemn recital—the set pieces we all knew by heart.

From the mountain we started an extraordinary ministry across Judea and Peraea. The number of followers were diminished and some of the women had left, temporarily. We walked the arid terrain and the dusty miles with him, and drank when he drank and ate when he ate. We also watched him pray but he did not pray as we did.

James said Jesus wanted to start a new religion, but I said maybe not, just to bring Judaism into fulfillment, and begin a new time showing the true way to God, for we had all strayed and needed correction. I asked him if he thought the sheep description was appropriate.

He thought for a moment and then said, insofar as it was a gentle and kind and loving image, yes, but Jesus expected us to be lions. We had to be lionhearted to do the work assigned, to face all the difficulties. How could we be meek and mild and humble? Who would listen?

I asked him why he thought these things, and he said Jesus had told them to be humble in our faith and conviction. Didn't I hear? I said there is so much he says, it is difficult to remember everything, but in time it comes back to me; when I sleep or walk or eat, I always hear his words. James agreed, but said he felt not all of us listen so openly. I asked what he meant, and he said, "Don't you sense the resistance, sometimes, coming from within? I feel there is one or more amongst us who no longer believes, or if he does, not fully. They still see themselves as true Jews, and Jesus as a denier of their faith."

"But Jesus had already nominated the twelve of us sitting on thrones judging the tribes of Israel. He did not discount anyone." I asked him if he doubted Judas Iscariot? And he said he did, and possibly the Zealot, and one or two others he would not name. I assured him all the others were resolute or why would they still follow him? He agreed, but Judas' discontent was mounting and Jesus must be warned against him. I told him Jesus would know this before we did, and was aware of it.

John then said had he saw that the twelve of us were not from the elite—including Judas—and that the backgrounds of most of the apostles were unknown, but presumed to be lowly, and how Jesus refused discipleship to those with higher social standing. How did Jesus choose his apostles, including Judas and Matthew and Simon? And the involvement in a momentous event such as the coming of the kingdom gave us a sense of worth and purpose, while the elite were opposed to upheaval. We were the lowest in the law and society. We had no stake in the system—religious or political—except perhaps Matthew. Was that why he chose us?

I said, "It's true. We were easier to attract, and his words did not incense us for we were not well learned, and a change of social order was appealing in his message, as well as the notion of a heavenly abode of similar people. But what of it?"

His words had strongest appeal to the lowest but the highest would never accept what he proclaimed. John said his message is for all men but only those with nothing to lose listened intently to him. I told him many Pharisees listened to him, but it was true, very few sympathized, but in time, it would be different.

The next morning, we waited for Jesus as he was still at prayer and slow to come out. I went to Mary of Magdala who was with us and I asked her about the woman taken in adultery. Was Jesus' action correct? She said she thought so, insofar as no sinner can accuse another of being a sinner. What hypocrisy is that? But I countered, "Adultery? It's a serious matter."

She said the woman was obviously ashamed and repentant, and Jesus told her to sin no more. "Jesus is very kind to sinners," I said. "Is that how we are all to be?"

She said she didn't know, but he was absolutely kind to women in general. She said, "I have never heard him berate a woman. He is so kind and generous to us. I'm not so sure if he would have been so kind if the male had been brought before him. But perhaps that's his point. Why was the male not accused too?"

She knew from custom that women were responsible for adultery, but Jesus had said any man that divorces a woman causes her to sin. How can people accept this? It was so contrary to our beliefs and customs. She then said, "People respond to his love and kindness, not to his observance of the law, for most of our laws are man-made, and the law of Moses is neglected."

Then Jesus came out and we continued our journey through Peraea. The crowds gathered when they heard he was coming, as he was so controversial, he could not be ignored. People listened and wanted to know what he was preaching and if he would heal and feed them—which he did. "It is true," they said, "he has the power of healing." And once they were healed and fed, most wandered off, not heeding his message of salvation, for they were temporarily satisfied.

He was preaching to the villagers, and, always out of curiosity and excitement, they came to see the man who it was said was from God, the great prophet after John, and taught by him, and they listened. They asked him continually, "What is the kingdom of God like?" And he answered in familiar parables. But when one asked him, "Who shall be saved? Who will enter the kingdom?," Jesus warned them that of the many, only a few will enter through the narrow gate, and not those who would be expected to enter.

"Do not expect to be allowed in just because you were taught and brought up as the children of Israel, because many who were not so taught will enter first, and they who say they knew him will be denied entry because they did not repent and take the warnings seriously."

They were peeved on this account. Outsiders would enter the kingdom before the chosen people? How could this be? But Jesus reassured them that they will come from all parts of the earth and from all levels and be with him and the prophets, for the first shall be last, and the last first.

At dinner, at the request of the Pharisees, he emphasized again that no one can think themselves worthy of heaven unless they repent. He told them that many important people were invited to a feast but were attentive to other business and refused to attend. They were subsequently denied entry, but the poor and sick and lame were let into the feast, and the invited were locked out because they shunned the invitation.

His whole slant that the first will be last was not directed at the Pharisees specifically, but at the children of Israel as whole, and the Pharisees scoffed at him with incredulity. What did he know? You could see it on their faces and hear it in their voices. But they kept their peace and asked why he stayed with sinners, which was itself considered a sin.

Jesus told them some parables, but the one that remained with me was the son of a rich man who foolishly spent his inheritance before the father had died and returned to the house as a poor, sick, and wasted man. But the father took him in, seeing his horrible state, and listened to his son berating himself. The father forgave him and brought him back into the house with much celebration. The older son then complained that he had never forsaken his father; why should his brother be treated like this? Why did the father never kill the fatted calf for his sake? The father reassured the older son his inheritance was safe, and simply said, "Your brother has returned from the dead; why shouldn't we celebrate?"

He said again that the lost sheep or the lost coin was most desirous to be found and any man or woman would leave what they had to find what was lost. So, he was saying he kept company with reformed sinners because they had come back to the fold and their gratitude was inestimable: because they had been forgiven much, they loved much.

Again, he knew the Pharisees were rich and emphasized that the rich were blinded by their wealth to their duties and priorities in life. He said, "You store up wealth and then you die, you look at the beggar and feel contempt, and when you are dishonest with small gifts given to you, greater gifts will be denied you." He then said, "Use money to build up friendship, and do not forget your duty to the poor, and with small responsibilities be honest, so that more can be entrusted to you."

With that, the Pharisees, who had been entrusted with guardianship and who squandered what had been given them as religious leaders and teachers, and who were wealthy and proud of it, strangely warned Jesus that

Herod was out to get him. Some may have been genuine, but they intended to frighten him away. Jesus just brushed it off, saying he was not afraid of that fox, and telling us again that he would die in Jerusalem, almost as if it were preordained.

Why was he so determined to die in Jerusalem? He said he loved the people there but they would stone him and would eventually kill him. Jerusalem caused him so much suffering, it was to be the prize of his ministry, but it was out of reach, and he could only lament its fate, which he prophesized as being desolate.

We left, and moved on until we rested again, and Jesus ate and drank a little and sat with us, and the women. He knew we were concerned about his safety, and our own, and so he spoke freely with us. He said that we will be looked after; we will be given gifts and all we need and we must persist; those who do not persist will fail. Those who tire of waiting will be lost; no one knows the hour whence the Son of Man returns; always be ready with the light burning and clothes at the door. He always referred to himself as the Son of Man, which was distinguishing, but not a unique title.

"No warning will be given, but for those who burn the light, they will be recognized and taken in. And those who hold out to the end in faith will be saved. But those who fall away when they knew of the coming, will be treated harshly."

But he told us many times that the way is difficult. I was excited to see how many were still willing to be with him, especially the women; none deserted him then, and were close to him. The twelve remained and were often alone with their thoughts of what the future held, but they understood that the future was what it was, and we would live each day in the glory of the coming of the Lord. But still we were only men, even if we were given extraordinary powers.

On another occasion further on, in a new town, Jesus was invited to the house of an important Pharisee and he took sustenance there, and at the same time a man with dropsy came to him at the door, and he asked to be cured. The Pharisees watched him for it was again the Sabbath, and this time Jesus asked them, "Is it lawful to heal this man today?" Surprisingly, they said nothing. And he cured the man, for it was the greater good.

He ate inside for some time. Again, we waited outside where the man had been and sat and rested; again we were surprised that prominent Pharisees asked him into their house. I asked Philip, "Why do they invite him when they hate him?"

Philip answered that they were also mystified by him. "They are not stupid people; they understood what he was saying and doing, and they took it personally, as they should. He put sinners and the infirm and the unclean above them, and their pride made them reject him. They had seen many miracles and still asked for more. They would never believe this itinerant preacher could possibly be the Messiah, even if he spoke the truth."

I went over to Mary and she sat with the women and she smiled at me. "Do you think the son should have been rewarded in his story?" I asked. "He acted foolishly, selfishly." She answered to the effect that in the law of love everyone can be saved. The righteous are justified and rightly rewarded, but for the wanderer, the lost, their position is precarious, and when they can see their faults for what they are, they can return to open arms. The dead for him are the spiritually dead.

Then she said something that the made me stop. "I am happy when he preaches of the lost and found, but I cry when he talks of the lost who will be thrown into fire. I watch the people and they back away. I am sure many joined him because they fear the torment, and equally they turn their backs, for it is not in the Scriptures."

I said she was right. The fire that he spoke of, the casting away, the gnashing of teeth for all time is frightful. He terrifies people who mostly do the best they can to keep the law which the Pharisees had adjusted for their benefit. Also, many thought they lived well enough—they loved their spouses and children, they worked hard, they did not cheat, they treated everyone with respect, occasionally they failed. Jesus was a divisive force, intending to have people question themselves and each other. I also said Jesus' law of love was not new to them. "He also tells people to repent, as did Jeremiah, John, and others, and they say he is just reciting them. Many have told me so."

She said, "But I trust in him. He has come to remind them of what they have forgotten—to be pure of heart."

It was true, the people argued that God, their God, had already conceived of their deliverance, and most did not contemplate the afterlife. But the afterlife meant no terror for people, whereas Jesus said those who could not be saved were banished into an eternal punishment and could never entre the kingdom. This idea was foreign to them, and many rejected it as not worthy of their Lord.

Jesus, it seemed to me, came with two new teachings: the kingdom of heaven and how it was imminent, and how people must look inward, repent, and change, in order to be included. For most people, however, the kingdom of heaven was meaningless the way Jesus preached it. It was taught to us that God's kingdom was to be established here on earth with Israel the leader of all nations. Was the heaven of Jesus the same as God's kingdom restored as the prophets had taught us?

Jesus said heaven was like "this and that," including the way people treated each other irrespective of who they were. He never spoke of the liberation and dominance of Israel, the return to the garden of Eden at the end of time, a restored kingdom here on earth. And that confounded many as they told me, and I took my thoughts to James and John often, and Matthew and Philip. John was actually worried about my faith, and James said we must obey him totally and put aside our doubts, for everything was new.

Also, I told Mary that other critics also said, "'Show us the signs of the Messiah—that he was predicted by the prophets, that he would be from the line of David, that he would bring in the messianic age, reunite the Jews into Israel, and reinstitute the Sanhedrin.' What can we say?" I asked.

Mary smiled again. "He often quotes Scripture to reveal the prophesies concerning himself. We have, as Jews, put the Lord into second or third place, behind everyday life, family, work, money . . . the worries and cares of this world. In this new life, Jesus wants us to show love to all, especially the poor and anyone in need, and to understand the true nature of sin, and be aware of sin, which is internal and damaging—something the Pharisees, with all their commandments, fail to realize."

"And this is God's kingship as is written in the Scriptures?" I asked.

"What is coming, no one knows—but he does," she answered.

"So, is the kingdom, that of our Father, the Lord God, the same as the kingdom of heaven?"

"There is only one kingdom," she said. "And yes, it is not of this world, but of the world to come."

I took in her answers; she had seen into the core of the fruit of the word. She continued, "We used to think our lives were God-centered, but they weren't. We recited our prayers and held the feast days and obeyed the law in outward observance; Jesus has come to reverse that, to put the Lord in his proper place and our relationship with him, and it is centered on how we treat our brethren and what dwells within us." I was satisfied with her explanation and told her so, and she put her head down to rest with eyes opened, and I left.

The following morning word came from Bethany that the brother of Mary and Martha was dying. Jesus then strangely said, "We will wait until he is dead before we proceed."

We knew and had seen how much he loved their family, and we looked to each other askance: why would he let Lazarus die? When word came again that he had died, Jesus made preparations to enter Judea and visit Bethany again.

It was dangerous for Jesus to go to Judea as many had set hard against him, but he was not concerned, and said that Lazarus was not dead but asleep, the same as he said of the daughter of Jairus. So, after two days, we made our way to Bethany where Jesus met again with Mary and Martha. Martha was in mourning and came to him and said that only if he had come earlier, he could have saved him. He assured them they would see the glory of God and he was late so that many may believe fully.

With that he ordered Lazarus to come out of the tomb, and many people ran away, and others yelled out, "What does he think he is doing?" Some fell back, and after they rolled the stone away, Lazarus appeared in his death wrappings which the people near to him quickly took away.

There was much gasping and disbelief, but the family fell into celebration, and Lazarus stood firmly and looked around him, and seeing Jesus, knelt and bowed his head, and Jesus raised him up.

Mary and Martha worried that Lazarus might smell, but Jesus dismissed it as a trite concern, typical of Martha. They all rejoiced and went into the house, and those present were, of course, stupefied, as we were all overcome by this feat. This man was not sleeping as the others may have been; he was truly dead and now walked amongst us. This was a demonstration of his heavenly power, and he turned to us and said, "I am the resurrection and the life; he that believes in me shall never die."

What man could have power over death? Surely, all could see he was the Son of God. We did not need this proof, but others did, most of whom already believed, but some sent messengers to the authorities in Jerusalem of what he had done, believing still in Jesus' wickedness and deceit and his league with the demons.

That night we marveled at what we had seen. Jesus stayed with Mary and Martha and Lazarus and we found lodgings nearby. The people were generous and fed us and let us wash. When we had settled, I went to Andrew and asked him if he believed what he had witnessed today. Without doubt, he did. But I said, "Who will believe us when we tell those who did not see what had happened? They will think we are mad or charlatans."

Andrew answered, "You worry about the future too much. A man can see without his eyes." He said again, "He had to do it because after all his healing they still held back, but now, surely, they must believe. He said it was for us, but no, it was for them, and all who come after them."

I smiled and sat near my brother. "This is such an age to be alive," I said. "Such a time has never been seen—the return of the kingdom. We must prepare, so that the Lord God can be truly honored. But many will reject us; it will not be easy, and I fear that what he says of his death will also be our fate. Our lives are intertwined like the loops of a fishing net."

"Yes, brother," Andrew said. "There is much still ahead. When his ministry ends, ours will begin and end the same. But like him, we know what is coming, and we go gladly to spread the word and accept our fate, for his word is life, and hence we must prepare the way and bring the chosen to the feast, for we have accepted the assignment."

And so, it was. The Scriptures were to be reignited and the kingdom returned and opened to us, for Jesus took us out of the desert of our apathy and timidity, into the oasis of a paradise, where evil will be defeated and the messianic age would be fulfilled, and everything restored to its rightful place. He had indeed come to fulfill the Scriptures. But I was perplexed why so many did not accept what he preached.

Unfortunately, word had reached Jerusalem of Lazarus' resurrection. It was feared that both Jesus and Lazarus were in danger as Caiaphas, the chief priest, wanted to cease all talk of resurrection performed by this man. The word was that Caiaphas said the people were confused and uncertain and told them if they turned away from the authorities to follow Jesus, they would be punished by God, and perish. So, it was better to kill one man than a nation. This was the decision of the Sanhedrin.

As a result, Jesus did not return to Jerusalem then but went on to Ephraim. We undertook an arduous missionary journey which we knew would then lead back to Jerusalem, eventually. We traveled through Samaria, along the Galilean border where many pilgrims for the Passover were headed towards Jerusalem, to Peraea and west across the Jordan through Jericho, Mount Olivet and thence, finally, back to Jerusalem.

13

HOSANNAH

THERE WERE SOME IMPORTANT EVENTS on this journey that I want to relate. We were aware the end was near, but Jesus delayed his final journey to Jerusalem. There was more he wanted to tell us before he departed. When we had reached the border of Galilee and Samaria ten lepers stood some distance away and shouted at him to take pity on them. He told them to present themselves to the priests as was the custom to see that they were cleansed. A little later one returned, a Samaritan, who gave thanks. Jesus asked: "Weren't there ten of you? Why is only one, a foreigner, thankful?"

He told the man his faith had cured him. Again, he emphasized to us that with faith we could move mountains. It was joyous to hear, because we had not numbers or weapons, but faith was our shield and our fighting arm, and we all felt strengthened by this invisible power when he spoke. And again, he emphasized and repeated that the table was prepared and it would be the most unlikely who would be welcomed to the repast.

About this time, I was walking with Simon the Zealot, and he suddenly asked why we walked around so much and did not consolidate our gains. I told him it was the best way to spread the word to all the people, but he said we lose some and gain some, and we should keep in one place, and let the people come to us. "And then we can let the town grow into a city and the city into a nation of believers."

He also asked why Jesus was not willing to set up fortifications and defend his people. He said he understood the Pharisees when they said that no number of miracles would convince them that Jesus was the chosen one, because he did not fortify Israel against the Romans, nor protect people against their enemies.

I had wondered what Simon had been thinking all these days, because he was mainly silent. Now I could see what his hesitancy was about. He wanted to see the days of the kingdom prepared in the regional arena, in a real change of political circumstances as foretold in the Scriptures, not just wandering and curing here and there, but to lay a physical foundation for the coming of the kingdom, built on a type of nationalist and religious fervor. "Had Jesus come to fulfill the Scriptures or not?" he asked.

I could not answer him but a little further on Jesus met with some Pharisees in a small town in the far north and their timely words were instruction to us all. They asked him simply, "When will the kingdom of God come? You speak of the coming kingdom, yet there is no sign the kingdom that Daniel prophesized is near."

Daniel had foreseen the domination of Israel over all others when the Son of Man would come in glory to his kingdom. But Jesus disappointed them, and, at the same time, avoided their trap to proclaim that he had come from God to usher in the kingdom as a type of religious-political leader by simply saying that the predictions were already being fulfilled, and hence avoided both treason and blasphemy. But complete fulfillment had to be delayed, for first he must be rejected, killed, and after three days arise again. But we were still not sure what he meant, and like the Pharisees, were left guessing.

He seemed to be saying that he would come again and the second time he will gather the righteous, those who believed and followed him, into his kingdom, as predicted by the prophets. And he told us later that there will be signs like lightning across the skies and all will be certain of the day and one will be taken in, and one left behind.

When I asked, "Where, Lord? Where will this happen?," he answered to look for the vultures, for there the dead will be. And he said no more then.

He went to be alone, and two Pharisees, seeing us without him, came over and sat with Andrew and myself. What did they want? They were friendly and polite and didn't mind being seen with us. We shared some food and drink which they brought and unwrapped. Most of the others moved away but I stayed to see what they wanted.

One spoke. "Many are fooled. It is easy to trick the unlearned, the naïve. He is about promoting himself, and he is deceitful. But we are not so easily fooled. Only God raises the dead. So, either he is God, or he is a charlatan. Either way he is condemned—for we know he is not God."

Then I wanted to move away, but the other one held my arm. Andrew insisted we leave. "We know how he raises from the dead. The same as all magicians. He is not even a prophet, just a magician and a blasphemer, and must be dealt with for deceiving the people and taking their money. Leave him before it is too late."

With that we turned away and joined the others, and the two Pharisees remained, looking after us. I turned back to them and said, "He was right when he said not to cast pearls in front of swine." With that they looked furious, twisted their cloaks around them and performed a curse.

Jesus did not see it; the others asked about what they wanted. We refused to tell them and said that Jesus was right when he said the Pharisees and Sadducees and scribes would unleash a fury against him, but they would not preform it themselves. They wanted the Romans to do their work so that Jesus' followers could not blame them. And they were turning the people against him in Jerusalem.

It was becoming obvious to us that these early days must pass before the kingdom would come. These were the preliminaries because the generation was resistant to his message. There would be no dispersion of the Romans, no true love of neighbor except by the few who followed him, and the many to come later.

Sometimes his words frightened us. Jesus spoke of the future but at the same time demonstrated how important the present was, for men must turn, and turn immediately, but the power of evil was well established and had blinded them and they were slow to accept.

And again, he told us that the kingdom was at hand and many will see it established in their lifetime. So, it was puzzling; perhaps he himself was uncertain which it was to be.

He told us so much in so short a time, it was hard to take it all in, and again, some would be forgotten. And it was then I realized we needed to record some things lest we forget them as they happened. But the idea passed as he continued.

He told a story to us as we rested about a judge who ignored the pleas of a woman to bring justice to her adversary. The judge was not wise or compassionate and did not care about her pleading, until, through persistence, he gave in to her in order for respite. We thought that God will dispense justice, unlike the judge, not through pleading, but through necessity. Matthew agreed that we should never stop asking of the Lord, but I disagreed, since the Lord could not be compared to the lazy judge.

And then he told another story, as he could see into our hearts, and there were many around. He said there was a Pharisee and a tax collector, and both went to the temple to pray. The Pharisee went to the front and proclaimed himself free from sin and a keeper of the law and even thanked the Lord for not making him a poor and destitute sinner. The tax collector humbly beseeched the Lord to have mercy on him. Who pleased the Lord the most? Some answered the Pharisee because he kept the law and was righteous, and the tax collector could not be heard because he betrayed Israel, and was a sinner.

But Jesus said all will be reversed. The Pharisee boasted of his privilege and adherence to the law but underneath he kept secrets not revealed, while the tax collector was honest and humble and open, and did not try to justify himself. He was pleasing to the Lord.

The Pharisees were important men, as were the scribes and priests and Sadducees; they interpreted the law and showed us the way to please the Lord and honor Israel. Were we to abandon them completely? Jesus had already shown us that not all of the Pharisees were unworthy and many were truly affected by his teachings, and seeing themselves reflected in his words, were repentant and chastened.

The people had to choose: the Pharisees and priests, or this man Jesus? It was not easy for them. By exposing the Pharisees, Jesus hoped to open the people to the true meaning of the Scriptures and how they were to be fulfilled, but many doubted him, even after what they had seen and heard, because of the Pharisees.

I asked Matthew, "How evil are the Pharisees, really? As evil as he says? They are men of God and communicate with him. And many are true servants."

"He despises them," Matthew answered. "They stand for everything he has come to destroy and set right."

Then a rich man came to Jesus and asked again what he had to do to receive the eternal life of which Jesus spoke. The man was an important magistrate and quite wealthy, and Jesus could see this and told him simply to keep the commandments. The man said that he did that. So, Jesus then gave him an impossible directive: "Sell everything and follow me."

The man turned away, but Jesus said to him, almost in apology, "The rich cannot enter heaven unless they have sold everything and understand what is truly valuable. Their riches blind them to the truth. Can a camel pass through the eye of a needle?"

This image astounded us. Jesus was always presenting the people with amazing images but a camel and a needle! He could relate so beautifully to us, but then we saw how impossible it was to gain eternal life, for it wasn't just the wealthy who were camels—it was all men who were truly unworthy of heaven. But he assured us that he would, on our behalf, make the needle eye open so that not only a camel but a whale could pass through.

We knew he was demanding the perfect life, but who could live it, or sustain it, and on our own it seemed impossible. But we saw again how he rescinded the elevated in society as his disciples. And again, he told us, apart from the others, that he would be killed in Jerusalem by the gentiles, whom we knew to be Romans. And on the third day he would rise. Whatever he meant, we accepted, because no one could question him; only amongst ourselves did we debate.

"Why would he willingly and knowingly do this?" I asked John.

"Where is your faith, Peter?" he asked. We didn't know at the time, but we were prying into the very heart of his teaching which would become apparent after the event.

Then he told us again that heaven is like a man who employs workers in his vineyard and hires them at different hours of the day but pays them all the same, as promised. Was it fair that those who labored all day were paid the same as those hired in the last hour? We thought not, but could see that many will be saved in the last hour. And, he assured us again, our reward is safe no matter what tasks we were given or the time spent—and to be content with that assurance.

But was this God of which he spoke the God of the prophets? Of Moses? He seemed estranged to us. Had we not been revealed the God of heaven who had formed his covenant with the people of Israel? That's why the Pharisees and their followers could not accept Jesus. His propositions were too contrary to their teaching and what we all understood and anticipated. He was projecting a God we did not know, almost a foreigner, and it was illuminating but difficult to reconcile. For Jesus was saying his Father was our God, but seen as we did not see him.

At Jericho, on the way to Jerusalem, there was a major tax collector who was visible in a sycamore tree waiting to see Jesus, and as Jesus passed, he called to him to come down, and Jesus said he wanted to go to his home for a meal.

He was taken in graciously by the man who later promised to restore all he had stolen, as it was their practice to steal or take in excess of what was required. The people there asked us in surprise, again, why he ate with publicans and sinners. We told them that he made no distinction; all who were repentant were welcome in the kingdom of God. But firm in their ways and beliefs they left him, as the holy did not associate with the wicked, lest they become like them.

One man said to me, "He is too free and easy with the law and the Scriptures." I said he obeyed both but shed new light on their meaning and how they should be observed. With that he snorted, spat, and walked away covering his back with his cloak.

A little later Jesus took the twelve of us to a secluded place and we sat around him, and he said again, in warning and preparation, that he would be handed over to the gentiles, spat at, mocked, whipped, and put to death. Again, we protested but he said the Son of Man must be glorified.

It was preposterous; glorified with spittle and whips? What were we to do? Fight the Romans for him? He said first he would be put before the chief priest and the scribes for testimony, and they will find fault with him. But the Romans, we asked, what is he to them? He said the Jews wanted him crucified. The Jews did not crucify other Jews, so they wanted him to suffer terribly, and only the Romans could do it and the behest of the Herodians.

We were more distraught at this. The third time he had predicted his death and he was walking to Jerusalem to have it done. How could anyone think he was the Messiah if he let this happen? The Jews mocked him; the Romans mocked him. A dead seed of wheat can produce bushels, he assured us. It seemed so much was left to us; we looked to each other as mere mortals. Twelve unversed men to take on the salvation of the world? Again, John later castigated me for my lack of faith, but I told him it would take more than faith to achieve what he expected.

Before we left Bethany a man came up to me and called me "brother" and held me by the shoulder. He hugged me and put something into my hand. It was a sword. He held me by the shoulders and said, "Brother, whither you are going, you will need this. If he is the Messiah, you must protect him." I objected because I had never carried a sword, and I said the Messiah is from God and needs no protection. He disagreed, and said I should take it, because the Romans were violent, and to use it to protect myself and others, even if the Messiah can protect himself.

He then walked away, and I was left with the small sword which I should have thrown into the brambles but instead put inside my belt and covered with my cloak, and walked on.

Then, before we entered Jerusalem, we went to the Mount of Olives again, and Jesus sat and we rested, many of us, including some women, and always Mary Magdalen. And Andrew and John sat close to him and I a little back, but I stood, and Jesus looked at me and saw something, and he told me that what was coming could not be fought against.

He then said he was hungry and went to a fig tree, but there was no fruit for him. Some of the women held out some bread and nuts but he seemed distracted by the tree, held one of its leaves, and cursed it, saying that it would never bear fruit again. And then he returned and ate a little from the women.

I said to John, he was cursing those who did not believe in him, perhaps Jerusalem, as the tree that did not bear fruit. John thought he was cursing the whole of Israel including the Pharisees who did not serve men as they should.

Did Jesus really expect that everyone would turn to him and accept him and leave their lives behind, and all that had come to them in custom and tradition from the Scriptures and the synagogue—even if he were from God?

John said that was how things were. Not everyone would be saved, only those sent to him by the Father. And they must not be lost. It was his duty to collect and save those so sent.

Jesus then asked for a donkey, and one of the pilgrims said he could borrow his. There were many of us, hundreds of his disciples, and thousands entering Jerusalem for the Passover, and those who had been walking with us were curious, as they heard this was the man who rose Lazarus from the dead. We tried to keep close to him and Philip and Andrew took it on themselves to guard him.

When we neared the gates, we could see the excitement rising, and Jesus sat on the donkey, and his disciples in their enthusiasm began to proclaim to the gathering crowd the arrival of he who comes in the Lord's name, "the King of Israel, the son of David, Hosanna!" And there was general tumult as many joined in and sang out, for it was a day of jubilation, and the disciples lay down their cloaks and palm leaves in front of him, and it was quickly copied.

I remained next to Jesus and walked with the donkey watching for the Romans. I did not want the crowd to call him "King" or "Son of David," but they proclaimed him so—in jest or sincerity, I think it was fair to debate.

Jesus sat placidly on the donkey and entered the city not as a conquering hero on a stallion, as Pontus Pilate would later do that day, but as the humble servant of the Lord, and no threat to the great Empire. Jesus wept openly in the passion of the moment; when I asked him why he wept, he said he wept for Jerusalem, because he loved it, but it would deny and betray him.

But the crowd quickly dispersed and their attention was taken elsewhere for the general excitement was like a fever that ran across the crowd and left them suddenly. As such, the attention of the authorities was diverted and Jesus was left alone, and he made his way to the temple.

But there were Pharisees along the way too, for they knew he was coming, and they were more incensed than the Romans. One said to me, "They are all for him."

I replied, "He comes to serve, not to rule."

"Is this how the ignorant perceive the Messiah? The son of David, riding on a donkey, as a lowly servant? The world has gone mad."

It was dangerous because the Pharisees must have hoped that the people would have tired of Jesus and ignored or insulted him, but they had not succeeded in turning them away from him completely. But this demonstration of acclaim was impossible to interpret. Were they for him or against him? Had the Pharisees failed? Or had they succeeded after all?

I could see in the Pharisees' faces still a type of quiet determination, for they knew the crowds were fickle, and what was praised today would be torn down tomorrow. For the would-be messiahs came and went, and they saw Jesus as no different. But for the Sanhedrin, Jesus was at last in their grasp, and they would demand reparation for the damage he had caused both to them, their beliefs, their God and Israel, the temple, their traditions and customs, the people, and the law.

14

At the Temple

WE WALKED WITH JESUS to the temple where he sat amongst the scribes and priests and Pharisees and others who had come to pray, and they soon sat around him, and we tried to come between them, but they forced us away and we sat separated from him, but he seemed not to notice or care, and continued to preach to those listening.

Some seemed content to listen to him and to talk with him, because he was an extraordinary man and was diverse, and with an appealing personality, but most saw him as objectionable both in his manner and proclamations. Yet they allowed him to preach and listened closely for something to hang on him. Especially given his reception into the city, the Pharisees did not want to accuse him openly. But they knew when the enthusiasm ended, they could act. So, they waited.

Meanwhile, Jesus again saw the sellers in the courtyard and again he became incensed. Firstly, the elders asked him if he was aware that children were proclaiming him the son of David, and others had called him King. Jesus replied that if the people did not cry out, the stones would. Again, he confounded them, as he did not deny or assent to their accusations but affirmed his authority.

With that, they thought of other ways to trap him, but it was not necessary, for Jesus stood and walked quickly through to the courtyard of the gentiles where there was, as usual, commerce and money changing, and the selling of sacrificial animals.

It was busy and bustling, but Jesus made a knotted cord from his cloak and whipped the sellers and turned the tables over. He told all the sellers to disperse and accused them of turning the temple into a house of thieves. Such an attack attracted the authorities, but no action was taken then, and it was seen by all, but the guards did not respond. It was, perhaps, considered a minor incident, but it disturbed the peace and momentarily curtailed the buying and selling of the sacrificial animals, as well as denying the Gentile Jews the currency they needed to enter the temple.

It was also noted by the elders and priests who hated him that he should order others to leave, and spoke of his "Father's house" as if he owned the temple. When Jesus returned to them, they asked him, "You speak and act with such assurance. Who gives you this authority, teacher?"

He refused to tell them, saying simply, "You mistreated John the baptist and you will mistreat me because our words cause you offense, not because what we say is false. You did not understand John, and you do not understand me."

He then insulted them gravely, saying that tax collectors and prostitutes would enter heaven before them, because even though they had defied the law, some had accepted repentance through John's baptism, but not the priests and scribes; they would never accept. I was amazed that they did not fall on him then, because their faces changed and flushed, and their shoulders were raised in anger, and they turned, denouncing him loudly to each other.

I thought his action in the temple was rash, even violent, and could have been handled differently, especially as it alienated the Gentile God-fearers the most.

He then went on to tell parables which were pointed at the scribes and Pharisees and, at each ending, their tempers rose as well as their frustration. In the end, he said that the rejected stone will be the cornerstone of the new building of faith, and repeated what he said before, that the feast of heaven will be open to those who were never invited, for the invited have shunned the invitation. But even then, the man who enters without the correct spiritual garment or cleanliness will be cast out as well. Not everyone who calls out "Lord! Lord!" will be heard.

Then, from the courtyard of the gentiles, three came to see Jesus and asked Philip, who as at the entrance, if they could meet Jesus. Philip then went to Andrew who was closest to Jesus and asked him if they could meet. Some said the strangers were from Greece or Persia, but they were Gentile God-worshipers.

I went over to them, apprehensive, and Jesus did not move but remained seated and continued talking to the priests and people in parables. But he did recognize them and strangely was aroused and declared that his glorification was at hand, for the seed of his word had spread far and wide—for those who follow him will be honored, and his Father's name will be glorified.

And then, as many attested, the thunder clapped and a voice could be heard pronouncing God's glorification.

Immediately, the priests and elders rose and shouted that a man was seen on the balcony and must be arrested, for it was he who sounded the drum and shouted out. There was commotion as the guards were ordered to arrest the man, but no one had seen him except the priests, and no one was found. Some said they heard nothing, others that it was an angel of the Lord. But they all settled again, and Jesus continued to speak.

Meanwhile, the gentiles near me asked what he was talking about, and why he was so aroused to see them. I told them they were the uninvited of which he spoke, yet will be the first to be saved. They looked curiously and asked if they could talk to me. I agreed and we left the room for another, which was in a quieter area.

They said they passed a tree on the way to the city on Mount Olivet that people said was cursed by Jesus and had withered and died. All the pilgrims stopped there now in awe. Then they asked, "Why did he curse the tree?" Before I could answer they told me of a great king from Persia who had the ocean lashed a thousand times because it destroyed his ships to show his dominance over nature. Was it the same? I said it was not the same. Jesus could quell the storms and waves that troubled men but he spoke in symbols and images, and I believed the tree was Jerusalem and he cursed it because the people there did not listen to him and could not be saved, even though he was from God.

"From God?" they asked.

"Yes."

"Then he is divine?"

They asked if he did have power over the waves, would they ever disobey him? I told them the waves and rains and winds were at his mercy because he did not fear them, and his faith and self-belief were flawless and absolute, so there was nothing he could not do as he exerted extraordinary powers. They then asked again why he was so happy on seeing them at the temple. I said I believed it was because they were from outside, foreigners, and not born Jewish, and it was the Jews who had largely rejected him. I said that the word of God was open, and that they were evidence of the fruit of his labors—the new skins and wine of which he spoke.

They wondered at this, and at last one said, "Do you really think that non-Jews will follow him?" I said that one had converted before me; why not others? But they said they had not converted themselves but were brought up in the customs and traditions of the Jewish law, and it was different. They were not idolaters. What did he mean by "all men?" All those of Jewish faith including the Samaritans, for instance? Or those not of the Jewish faith?

I reiterated that non-Jews could be saved, and as the Jews rejected him, so others, such as the God-fearers of all lands, would take their place. With that they consented and continued on their way to the temple.

I also returned to the temple and found Jesus still engaged in preaching, and I could see some priests and leaders were closer to him; I thought they would try to kill him, but their expression told otherwise. They were listening with an open heart, and with eyes wide, they discussed with and questioned him. His opponents had moved to the back. Philip and Andrew were still near him but others were pushed further out. I could not get closer. But then Jesus stood and walked through the crowd to me, and said we should walk a while.

Outside, the crowds were teeming, and one could not find respite anywhere. The animals and dust and noise were intoxicating. Then a group came up to Jesus and said to him, "Rabbi, we know you are an honorable man and fearless, and you will tell us what is true to you, so tell us, should we pay our taxes to Rome? Is it lawful?" It was obviously a trap, an embarrassing one, for they had praised him first to make him feel important so as to commit himself to treason. But he asked for a coin and was handed one and asked whose image was on the coin, and they said, "Caesar's."

They waited for his response to catch him and report him, but he said, simply, "Then give unto Caesar what is Caesar's."

He handed the coin back and they were speechless, for again, he neither affirmed nor denied the duty to pay tribute but had answered the question. "You hypocrites," he said. "Your mealy mouth words try to hang me, yet my words open the world to the truth." With that he moved on and we moved with him and he caused a commotion as he passed by.

"There he is," could be heard. "The prophet from God. Some say the Messiah." And still others, "He's the servant of Beelzebub."

Then two Sadducees came to him through the crowd and asked him to sit inside a compound in the shade. He took myself and John, and we sat and rested in the portico but the crowd still mingled around us, some distance apart. The Sadducees did not believe in resurrection, unlike the Pharisees, as it was inconclusive what came after death, and most of us believed in a quiet life, without judgment. But the Sadducees knew Jesus preached about the afterlife and so asked him about it: a woman who marries her deceased husband's brother becomes his wife. At the resurrection, will she have two husbands?

Jesus sighed, and said that there would be new life just as Abraham and Jacob and Isaac are born anew, and men would become like angels, without human restrictions or relationships.

"How do you know this?"

"I have seen the glory of the Lord," he replied.

They stood back, afraid and hesitant. "He has seen heaven?"

He simply said, "As it is written, I have seen it," and walked away.

There was more movement and more discussion as he rejoined the street crowd, and the Sadducees had something more to tag on him. But then a teacher came to him humbly and with respect, and asked him politely, "What is the greatest of the commandments?," and Jesus repeated the Scriptures, that to love God wholly and your neighbor as yourself were the greatest. With all his answers his enemies could not find fault. The teacher said, "You are right, Rabbi. These are the greatest of the commandments, greater than the worship in the temple or all the sacrifices and offerings."

Jesus then looked at the man and told him he was near to the kingdom. But most did not ask to be instructed; they asked questions to set him a trap and drag him before the Sanhedrin, and he saw through them, and was at last finished with their games and pronounced damnation upon them.

He told everyone listening that the Pharisees had misled them: they did not teach by example. They loved to be feted and pampered and were well dressed and tasseled, and honored and sat together appropriately, and they hung great weights upon the people in terms of rules and laws without respite; they paraded their observances for all to see and admire, but he promised the people that whoever exalts himself shall be humbled, and the humble will be exalted. This was codified in the kingdom of God.

He then entered a sevenfold condemnation of the scribes and Pharisees as a culmination of his diatribe. For the religious leaders who were supposed to open heaven for the people to enter actually blocked the way for themselves and others, even as he, Jesus, came to open the door and show the way. They rejected him and clung to their outward observances.

Secondly, he condemned them for making converts to Judaism obey the law of man, that is, of the Pharisees, rather than taking them to God. He then condemned the practice of oath taking which was manipulated by the Pharisees and others to their benefit. He went on to condemn them for their taking oaths on the temple gold as binding, and not on the temple itself. He also called them hypocrites for the minutiae of their laws and observances while ignoring the essence of the law: justice and mercy, and that their self-obsession with their own laws blinded them to the central demands of Scripture and the commandment to love.

The Pharisees were like plates cleaned on the outside but putrid on the inside because they liked to parade as holy and righteous when in fact, they made the law self-serving, and were full of pomposity and sinfulness. He made stark images of their vileness which were even confronting for us. He said they were like washed tombs full of death and decayed bones.

Could any man stand this type of abuse? He despised them so much that in his controlled rage he committed them to perdition. We were astounded by this tirade and I, for one, felt like apologizing to him. Those so rebuked stood flabbergasted and tried to sneer at him, and walked away one by one as he was speaking, telling the people to close their ears.

They had come to the end with him. Even the moderates were horrified at his words, and many people, too, turned away in disgust.

One of the moderates, the same teacher who questioned Jesus about the greatest commandment who had listened closely but now was forced to turn away too, came over to me first, shaking his head. "Is this the way to win the people?" he asked. "After all, these are their religious leaders, the educated and learned in the law; the people respected them as close to God. So, if they were condemned, so were the people who followed them, as they had for generations. Were they to give over their leaders for this makeshift preacher who claimed to be from God? He did marvelous things and his words were healing, but to treat their religious leaders like this was like an insult to God who had appointed them, and to Israel, which they served."

I could understand him but assured him the Pharisees and priests and Sadducees were not without fault, and their pride kept their sins covered, and they were not the leaders they should be. They had perverted the Scriptures for their own ends and paid lip service only to the law.

The people were confused and even alarmed, and looked to their leaders for direction, for they rejected what they heard from Jesus in favor of the religious authorities, as was demanded. Now he called them washed tombs. They stood aghast. With that the Pharisee moved away to be with the others.

Then, as Jesus saw the temple treasury being filled with money and great sums being deposited by the rich, he located a poor widow entering from the corner who dropped two coins into the coffers and walked away humbly. Jesus was so impressed he told us, "She has given all she had, and her reward shall be great. The rich give what they can easily afford; where is the merit in that?"

After which Jesus decided to leave the temple and he walked towards the Mount of Olives for respite, and just the twelve went with him. Thomas, I think it was, exclaimed, looking back at the temple, how magnificent it was. Jesus was not impressed. He said it would all crumble and the stones would scatter on the earth like leaves in autumn. We wondered if he meant it as it was said, or if his meaning different.

We walked up the mountain and Andrew, John, James, and myself were with him when we rested with views of the temple. I asked him when this destruction will happen, and how we will know it is coming?

From other things that he had told us we were growing in understanding that Jesus would come again. This first visit may not have been as successful as he had hoped, but the second and last coming would establish the reign of the kingdom of God. But when? He didn't dismiss the question but answered in words we knew not. He described the time as harrowing. There would be the birth pains of events such as fires, earthquakes, famines, and floods; there will be many false prophets preying on the fears of the people; and we would be persecuted as we stood our ground, not knowing what to say, but the Lord would put words into our mouths, he assured us.

Then there would be a tribulation never experienced before—the sun and moon would lose their light as the last sign of the coming of the Lord, and the elect, those whom God has chosen, will enjoy the delights of heaven with him. From my memory, that was to be the sequence of events, but as I said, of what he spoke we knew nothing. But he assured us the events were imminent and we had every day to watch out for the ruination, and then his coming in power and glory on the clouds.

These were extraordinary scenes painted for us; some of the words were familiar from Scripture, but to hear them spoken in the voice of our

Master, and to watch his face as he spoke, was to be drawn into a whirlwind and depth of emotion impossible to describe.

He then settled what I had known all along; his words were unblemished opulence, sublime and everlasting, and yet no one wrote down a single one. How could we remember everything he said, word for word? And yet they must be preserved. We must somehow take his words to the next generation, and the next, if necessary. We sometimes discussed this, and some like John said everything could be remembered and passed by word of mouth. But I had doubts, since every day there was so much said and done, the details were escaping us already, as I asked them about the miracle of the man with dropsy: did the man enter the house or was he cured outside? There was no complete agreement. How many lepers were there, and so on?

Hence, I requested a scribe, one of the disciples, to carry parchment, ink, and quill and to record some details as we spoke to him in the evenings, but not to tell Jesus, because he would not allow it. And so, each day we recalled what we could, and carried it with us going back to the days when we first met him. We spoke together of what we remembered and when there was disagreement I took the majority view, or the view of the one most certain.

I was pleased we took this measure, but the scribe I cannot disclose, at his insistence.

15

THE FINAL HOURS

BEFORE WE LEFT, HE TOLD us to be watchful. He understood our concerns but told us to be like the five virgins waiting for the bridegroom to take to the wedding: they did not know the hour of his arrival, and one took extra oil for her lamp, but the other four did not think of it and their lamps were extinguished when the groom arrived, and they were bypassed.

And then he gave us a warning: he said much is expected of us, because we have been given much in way of insight and understanding and close contact. He said, "You who are chosen because of what you have already; much more will be given if you are fruitful, but being unproductive you will lose everything, even that which you had." I understood that to mean that Jesus expected much from us in way of discipleship, and we must not fail him, for we were indeed privileged to share his ministry with him, day and night. Our responsibility was therefore great, and we must not depart from the Scriptures as the Pharisees had done.

Finally, he stood up and spread out his arms and told us that like goats and sheep the peoples of the nations will be separated. The sheep will have entry but the goats denied because they did not treat their fellow man well in spite of the commandment. Those adherents, even on the simplest acts of charity, would be saved because their acts were done as if for him in true faith. For the kindness and sympathy that we showed to those who have not and have suffered and are burdened will be repaid in heaven. He then called us friends and not servants, and we responded in kind, and said we would not fail him.

We returned to the disciples and we went back to the city but I noticed Judas Iscariot was missing. They said he went ahead to invest the money. Jesus sent myself and John to prepare the room for our supper. We did not know at the time but the Sanhedrin was conniving on how to arrest Jesus. The people were both for and against Jesus, but to avoid a scene, they decided to arrest him in the evening, quietly, and present him as a blasphemer the next day. They must have wondered if in the night the Pharisees' soldiers could recognize him, and needed some way to identify him.

We knew the time was near, and after John and I had prepared the room, I saw Judas return; I asked him where he had been. He seemed downcast and asked why Jesus always took myself and John and James with him for special counsel, even the women, and never bothered with him, or others. I knew Judas was jealous, and he had abilities and ambitions. His voice was resonant and his figure imposing, and he remembered a great deal, and knew the Scriptures. He also asked me why I never asked him about his opinion on things that Jesus did and proclaimed.

I wasn't expecting this, and I told him we all had our place and our duties. But he said he had more to offer to the Lord, but he never confided in him, and the Lord's secrets were kept hidden, but to me, Peter, he revealed everything. He didn't understand why Jesus had assigned him a lower place, for he understood him well and what he said.

Jesus could see us talking in this way but kept his distance. He then rested a while and Judas sat with me on a stone and I could see his eyes fill with water. I looked at his face and it was striking, well proportioned, with a thick strong beard and piercing eyes, and his lips moved carefully to pronounce his words deliberately. We shared some bread and I asked him about his family and he spoke a little about them. He had a wife but no children and both parents were Sadducees, but his wife and parents all disowned him when he decided to follow Jesus.

He told me they were raised in the law and had attended school in the synagogue and adhered to the Scriptures, strictly obeying all the laws, but when Jesus called him, he felt a dire obligation to answer as he gave a new perspective—breakaway announcements that were well met, and a need to be with him, and took in all his words and actions and made them his own, because he wanted to be like him, and sacrificed much to follow him.

He ate and swallowed hard. I asked him what impressed him most about Jesus. He thought for a moment and conceded that it was "his insights into the human heart." He said he was "otherworldly" and feared no one except the Lord God, and could see what other men were blind to. And then I asked him what was in his heart. He stopped and looked distressed but said nothing, and quickly regained composure. "He should not have put me aside, because I loved him and wanted to be close. He put women before me. And what he asks is too much of us, this cloak of perfection, and yet he has not freed Israel, which I also love."

I told him that James and John had been rebuked for wanting places of honor next to him in heaven, and he never left any unattended. Keep the faith, keep the peace, and follow him. But he said he may leave the twelve and buy a field for farming after the Passover, and that he would not be missed. He stood abruptly and left, and then Jesus and the others rose too, and we all walked on to the town and the room which was prepared.

Once inside, we lounged around the table and were happy enough, but Jesus had asked that no lamb be prepared which was essential for the feast, but we drank a little and ate and conversed freely. The room was large with columns and arches and a cold stone floor, and was sparsely furnished. There was a single window on to a courtyard.

We reveled a little and John lounged next to Jesus and rested his head on his shoulder. Then Jesus said that he will be betrayed this night. I asked, "How? Betrayed? By one of us?"

He said the priests knew him well enough but one of us would seal his fate with a kiss. We all denied such a thing. I asked how the kiss was betrayal. And he answered it was conceit that broke the bonds of trust between compatriots—not hate or enmity, or even riches.

"It can't be one of us," I said, and I did not appreciate the allegation or that Jesus would not identify the traitor, but I insisted that he would be punished.

"Peter, listen to yourself. His punishment was having been born and what God has ordained let no man put aside." I realized then it was Judas Iscariot, even though others felt it was the Zealot. I looked to him, and he stayed calm and even appeared surprised at the news. But I wondered why Jesus never named him. Did he know it would be Judas, or just suspected it?

Jesus then took bread and wine and held them up for us to eat and drink, saying, as he had before, that this was his body and blood, the blood of the new and final covenant with God, which was to be offered for all sins. Was he saying he could forgive the sins of the world? His flesh and blood would be sacrificed to do this? Who was demanding this? The Lord God himself?

We looked at each other, not knowing what his words meant. We were eating his flesh like that of the sacrificial lamb offered at Passover, and I remembered the words of John the baptist to Andrew, that this was the Lamb of God, the perfect sacrifice. Jesus had told us before that he was the bread of life, and eating and drinking his flesh and blood would bring eternal life. But the drinking of blood was strictly forbidden, as we had already discussed. We hesitated, but accepting that it was wine, and not blood, we drank.

It was disturbing but he was so absorbed in the ritual we dared not question him and did as he asked. Again, he said the bread was his body, and we ate.

When the supper ended, he took some of us to the Mount of Olives again and to the garden known as Gethsemane, where I met the phantom of my shame. The Lord said we would all fall away from him but he would come again to Jerusalem. I promised him, foolishly, that I would never leave him and would die for him. "But deny me, you will, three times before the cock crows twice."

I said, "Never, why would I?"

But he only said, "Stay a while as I pray." And he shook all over and perspired freely.

We heard him praying in the distance: he was distraught, and then we fell asleep as the day had been long and exhausting, and he returned and found us there and asked couldn't we stay a little while with him? And sadly, this happened three times, and each time he returned to find us asleep and he addressed me personally, asking why I couldn't share this hour with him.

He was disappointed and I felt ashamed and could not answer because the closing of my eyes shut out the world and I did not want to be called anymore. I wanted peace and to be left alone and not to be involved with what was coming, and the people had turned and nothing was as it should be. The prophet from God had been rejected. It was all a failure. He was not to be proclaimed as the Messiah, only by a handful, which was useless.

But then Jesus gathered his strength and said, "Here they come," and a group of armed thugs came from the Sanhedrin, and Judas came up to Jesus and said simply, "Rabbi," and kissed his cheek, and they seized him. Jesus said he would go without resistance, and said their weapons were for revolutionaries—was that how they described him in the Sanhedrin?

Instantly, I took out the sword I had been carrying and rashly slashed the face of a guard. But Jesus admonished me and told me to put it away, and he knelt and joined the man's wound. He looked at me and said, "Simon Peter, the sword cuts both ways."

With that they took him away, and once the shepherd was gone the sheep scattered but I remained with him, walking behind him with John until we reached the courtyard of the high priest where people mingled, and they took him inside and stopped me from entering, so I sat by a fire as they interrogated him, and John had vanished also.

After some time passed the chief priest came out to the balcony and announced that Jesus had condemned himself and declared he was the Son of God. We later heard from some of the priests that he had refused to defend himself against the charges, but then proclaimed he was the Messiah in front of Caiaphas. They found that was sufficient to warrant the death penalty. The people in the yard barely moved. They looked up and remained silent. The moment he prophesized had come.

At the same time a woman came to me and said she had seen me with him. I denied it, and said I did not know him. She said again I was one of them and again, more forcefully, I denied it. Finally, someone said I was a Galilean and must be with him, and this time I swore I did not know him. And the cock crowed twice and I was aware of the prediction, for I had betrayed him as surely as any other.

My cowardice was numbing. Yes, I was afraid of them, afraid for my life and did not want to be involved. But I had betrayed Jesus as he said I would. I wept bitterly, for cowardice is a horrible, demeaning realization that swelled like a debilitation in my body and heart. How could I live with myself then with this degradation—this monstrous flaw of character revealed?

My Master had been betrayed by his chosen one, the one that he respected the most. I wanted to hide and never be seen again, never to return to my family, to wander in life as a miserable miscreant, and I wept tears of sour remorse and shame and could not stop.

Everything he had given to us, everything he had taught us over the years, the call to be a witness, and I had failed him, and I remained paralyzed with dread.

What happened next was revealed later by priestly sympathizers. He was taken before Caiaphas and then to the governor Pilate who was in Jerusalem. The reports of what happened came to us over time, but I can relate now on witness reports what was said, mainly from some of the affiliate priests.

Jesus was before Pilate. He, Pilate, sat on a chair like a throne with a table holding wine and fruit. The room was open to the outside, airy, and cool. He stood and went over to Jesus who had already been beaten by the priests and Pharisees. It was early morning and the first dawn appeared. Pilate went over to the window and then came back and confronted the priests and spoke to them in Arabic. "What is this man accused of?"

"Blasphemy," they answered.

"Then you deal with it," he said, walking slowly across the room with arms folded.

"We want him crucified," they said.

"Why? Because he has blasphemed? Not against Rome's gods or emperor."

"He is a danger to Rome."

"Really? Let's see." He stood near but not too close to Jesus. "They say you are the king of the Jews. How do you answer?"

"You said it, not I."

Then the priests said, "The people call him the king and the Son of David—the Messiah. Aren't you afraid of an uprising?"

"We have laws," he said, "Roman laws, and we stand by them for the peace, both internally and externally. We do not crucify innocent men. You have your laws; he's not our problem."

Then the chief priest went up to Pilate and said, "We work together to keep the peace. The Herodians, the Sanhedrin, and the Romans, we support each other, for the times are volatile. If you do not support us, it weakens the pact, and revolts may erupt and be difficult to deal with. We want him crucified."

"He must have really violated you. He is one of your own, and a prophet."

"We have tolerated his insults and blasphemy for years and now there has to be a reckoning. We will have our day of justice."

"If I have him crucified it will not be by Roman law, so I will wash my hands of his blood."

"Then we accept responsibility for his punishment."

"He says he is your king."

"Only Caesar is our king." With that they had cornered him, and he ritually washed his hands.

It was said that he was then taken to Herod who thought the affair amusing and asked Jesus to perform some miracles before returning him to Pilate, telling him to do what he must with him.

Pilate knew that at the Passover one prisoner was released, and he recognized that Jesus was popular and the people might ask for his freedom. That way he could save his life.

"I am not caring one way or the other. I crucify many men and think nothing of it, but I will not adhere to this and nothing will be recorded, but you will have your crucifixion—we will execute him as a Zealot, a rebel, and mark him as 'King of the Jews,' as a warning."

With that the priests and chief priest and Pharisees all congratulated each other. "From here our guards will take him in," he said, and they bowed and went down into the courtyard, for they knew about the ritual release, and must persuade the people not to release Jesus.

I was in the courtyard when Pilate presented to those waiting, and mainly they were subdued. The priests and their followers were in the front of the assembly and were already calling for his crucifixion. Then Jesus appeared battered and bleeding, head up but gaze cast down. He held a miter and wore a crown of thorns. I could not see any of the apostles anywhere. It was wrenching to watch our Master so treated, and deserted.

Pilate then asked if they wanted to release Barabbas or Jesus, and there was no spontaneous outburst until the priests called out to release Barabbas, and they turned to the people and incited them to call for Jesus to be crucified. Those nearest the priests complied but further back they were silent, for many had experienced the power of Jesus and were afraid, but also, they knew he was a good man and were reluctant to agree.

But as the morning sun grew so did the temper, and gradually, at the insistence of the priests, they called for his crucifixion, because they wanted to impress the priests, but still many did not cry out, but cried. And I looked at Jesus, and he was calm and seemed without pain although he had been severely flogged. His eyes were still all-seeing and his expression composed, and looked beyond his ordeal to some distant, tranquil reprieve. Pilate again washed his hands in front of the crowd and Jesus was led away.

Finally, the Pharisees had their time, the time they had waited for for years, and they had withstood the potential upheaval of their religion, and congratulated each other, and the crowd dispersed with mixed feelings— satisfaction, guilt, and remorse were all evident.

I remember Jesus saying where he was going, we could not follow, but we would follow afterwards. And when he was brought to the street his cross was presented by the soldiers; strangely, they held it upside down for better balance. But it was then turned and straightened and one from the people, a Simon of Cyrene I was later told, was forced to help carry the cross. I parted because I could not watch the execution in public, and I wore my cowardice like a sackcloth, and I slunk away not knowing what to do next because without him we were lost.

And that was the last I saw of him that day.

16

The Empty Tomb

I THEN RETURNED TO OUR LODGINGS and found some of the disciples there, including James and Andrew. Saddened, I tried not to think of his suffering but of the time when he was with us and called us friends. I asked James what he would do then, and he said he didn't know. I said I would likely return to my home in Capernaum and return to fishing.

Meanwhile, Joseph of Arimathea had solicited Pilate for the body of Jesus on the evening of the crucifixion, according to the priests. Pilate had no qualms, but it was an unusual request. The Sanhedrin, however, were furious as they wanted the body treated like that of a common criminal and thrown into a pit, anonymously, to be devoured by animals. But Pilate was agreeable or nonchalant to the request seeing he had found no fault with the man and wanted the tiresome affair finished. Some members of the Sanhedrin, however, were apparently relieved as they insisted Jesus be given a proper Jewish burial, and be buried before sunset.

The Sanhedrin, overall, castigated Joseph, and rumor was he was put into prison but escaped back to Arimathea, as he was wealthy and probably bribed the guards. Joseph was a member of the Sanhedrin, and one of those who opposed the crucifixion, by all accounts, and the tomb that was prepared for Jesus was to be his own.

It is also said that the Sanhedrin told Pilate to seal the tomb because the suspicion was that his disciples were wanting to steal the body and say he has risen. Pilate also placed guards outside the tomb at their request.

The eleven of us—Judas was nowhere to be found—were staying in Jerusalem in the same place and in the morning, after the Sabbath, Mary

Magdalena came back excited and told us she and two other women, another Mary and the mother of James and John, and some others went to the tomb to anoint the body, but found the sealing stone rolled back, and the guards gone.

Mary told us, breathlessly, that the tomb was empty, and she then saw Jesus outside. She said Mary and Salome had remained but had fled in fear when we told them the tomb was empty, but they had not seen him.

I looked at John and his face flushed, and immediately we set out to see for ourselves. And when we got to the tomb the huge stone had been rolled back and the guards had gone. There was no one there, and the tomb was empty except for the strips of linen which had been wrapped around the body.

I asked John what he thought had happened, and he said, "He has risen, as he said he would." I was hoping it was so, but did not celebrate, and waited for confirmation, for the idea was preposterous, and was surely not what he meant when he was alive, that he would come back from the grave.

On returning to the room where we all met, I asked Mary if she was sure it was Jesus. She said it was, but at first, she wasn't certain, as he looked different; he looked younger and less afflicted and his face was hard to define. He told her not to touch him but to tell us he was going to the Father, but would first meet with us.

My wife, Joanna, had joined two days after she heard he had been crucified, and as she rested after the journey, she asked me bluntly why I had not stayed with him during his suffering. "Surely, it would have been of comfort to him to have seen you, Peter."

"I couldn't bear the sight," I said, but truly I was afraid for my life, and she knew it.

"What of the others?"

"Only John," I said.

"Maybe there will be time to make reparation," she answered. "Has he truly risen?" she asked. I said I didn't know but the body was missing and Mary Magdalen said she saw him. "Then it is true," she said without hesitation. "Can't you see? The end of time is here."

I answered I wanted it to be so, but how could it be?

"He was one with God," she said.

"Then why did he need to suffer at all?" I asked.

"He suffered for us. He gave his life that we might be free from death."

"You have discussed these things?" I asked.

"We have; in our house, the community has grown and when we heard of his death, we mourned but knew he would come again, as he said."

"But this resurrection. Is it what he meant by rebuilding the temple?"

"Look and see," she said. And then there came a knocking at the door and Andrew entered and told us that two disciples had seen Jesus.

Joanna and I went outside and there was a small milling of the disciples. "They've seen him." And two came forward excited and said they saw him on the road to Emmaus and broke bread with him.

"What did he say?" I asked.

"To go and tell you that we saw him."

"Are you sure it was Jesus?"

"Not at first, because we heard he had been crucified. But we talked, and he was calm and friendly and we invited him back to our lodgings for the night. At supper he broke the bead and blessed it, and gave it to us, and suddenly I recognized him as he stood up—Jesus of Nazareth." But Clopas, as he was called, knew nothing of our supper together; why should this act reveal Jesus to him? Why did Jesus reveal himself to them at all? Why was he on the road?

I thanked them and offered them food and a place to rest for the night. I said to Joanna, "He is everywhere; why not here? Why didn't they recognize him at first? Then suddenly he was apparent to them. The same as with Mary."

"Perhaps he didn't want to terrify them and kept his face concealed," she said.

We stayed together and then decided we must return to Galilee. We made preparations and all of us would walk separately so as not to attract attention, and the eleven must disperse. We slept on the floor and benches, wherever we could find a space and kept close to keep warm. And in my sleep, I saw him, as clear as day, sitting on one of the benches not far from me. He sat and looked around and was relaxed and contained, and looked at me and I was not afraid, but held out my hand but could not reach him. He put some writing in my hand, it was from Scripture, from Joel and David. He told me to read it to the disciples.

And then, that night, there was wind and the air penetrated the room where many of us were gathered locked in and secure, and it was dark and, suddenly, he stood before us, Jesus, the risen Christ stood before us, and wished us peace.

We were, of course, afraid, and the hairs on our head stood up, and we could not at first believe it was Jesus in physical form, but he assured us it was he who had risen. And he sat with us as we were all speechless and he ate with us and we talked a little at first. He was disappointed that we had not understood what it was he said, that after three days he would rise and the temple of his body will be rebuilt. He then told us that he will leave us, but remain with us forever in spirit. We were to go to all the world and preach the message of the coming kingdom and the need for repentance. But I asked him why he had to leave. Surely, to remain with us and continue the preaching would be better as everyone would now believe in him.

But he told us it would change nothing, as men believed what they wanted to believe and closed their hearts, and our work was to continue what he had started, for he had to return from whence he came. Whatever we gained on earth was won in heaven, and what was lost was also lost there, such was our authority. But we were to fulfill the Word and preach to all nations in their language, and we would be given the gift of tongues by the Holy Spirit.

We still wondered if he was a spirit and not of body. As it happened, Thomas was not present, and when we told him of the event, he said he would not believe unless he touched the wounds of Jesus. And on the next appearance, after a few days, Thomas was present and Jesus showed him the healed wounds, and he then exclaimed, "My Lord and my God," to the amazement of all, because it was, as we knew, a Roman greeting reserved for the divine emperor.

But it was also significant because Jesus had supplanted the emperor as man and God. Jesus then blessed those who had never seen but still believed. By then we were convinced that Jesus was body and spirit joined, signifying the real presence of life after death, as was foretold by Scripture.

After we had eaten Jesus said to me, "Simon, do you love me?" I replied that he knew it. He then said, "Feed my lambs." He asked again and I reaffirmed, and he said to tend his sheep and one more time he asked, and I said yes, with some consternation. I was amazed that after denying him before his death he still vaunted me and valued my love for him. And he said, "Feed my sheep." I could only assume he meant the disciples now and those to come; to lead them in the truth and light he had shown us.

He then said he must leave us but would remain with us all days, even to the end of the world, and we were to follow him to Bethany where he was to ascend to God, and then for us to return to Jerusalem to wait for the Holy

Spirit. We did not know what he meant by the "Holy Spirit" or to "ascend," but we knew rightly that the floor of heaven was situated above the ceiling of the sky. Was he to enter heaven that way?

So, he then took a few of us, John, James, Andrew, and others to Bethany where he stood on the Mount of Olives, and the breeze blew through his hair and clothes, and he looked as I remember him when he had been earlier transformed, and he turned his face into the sun, and he closed his eyes and for some time remained still with his hands out in front of him, and then said: "Look!," and pointed to the clouds in the sky gathering and swarming in a frenzy. We looked, and then he was gone. We searched for him and asked each other what had happened, and we returned to Jerusalem without him.

I asked the others if they had seen anything, and they said they hadn't, but that he must have ascended or was otherwise taken away.

17

BAPTISM BY FIRE

JESUS HAD ASKED US TO wait for the Holy Spirit and that was also a daunting prospect, for what form would it take? Word had spread about the empty tomb and the sightings of Jesus, and many people came and gathered around where we stayed, but no authorities or Romans came near. In the room where we waited day after day, the numbers swelled until we had to close them out—about fifty were present at any one time.

Mary, the mother of Jesus, had joined us, and she was accorded special place with James, her son. She was thought to have been at the cross but denied it. She said she was there but not close. She had only just arrived from Galilee and could not bear the sight of her suffering son. But Mary of Magdala had been there, much to our chagrin. She did not ask where we were, but could sense our remorse.

When Mary arrived, she asked Mary Magdalen for a description of what happened. Mary broadly outlined the way of the cross ending with the nailing and raising of the cross. He suffered for three hours according to the sun, and spoke little but to ask for water. But he did say to John, who was there, to behold Mary his mother, and for Mary ("woman") to behold her son. She thought Jesus must have been confused and delirious. But I remembered him saying something similar in Capernaum.

There were also other women at the cross. But he also said to one of the others also crucified with him that he would be with him in paradise. She said she had never heard Jesus use the word "paradise" before, and was sure he was beside himself because the scene was so removed and remote from any such place; Gotha was an abomination. Lastly, he said, "Father, why have you abandoned me?" And finally, for all to hear, "Into thy hands I give up my spirit."

I asked her if Jesus asked where his disciples were. She said no, he said nothing about them, except to John, but he took much comfort in the women being there.

She said they had paid men to take down the body which was very difficult and wrenching to watch, and Joseph quickly transported it to his tomb where it was not washed or anointed but merely wrapped in cloth. And Joseph and she both departed as the soldiers prepared the stone seal.

Jesus' mother then said that John took her in when she arrived in Jerusalem, and promised to care for her hereafter, for her husband, Joseph, had passed away a year earlier and her daughters and sons were scattered, except for James, who was with her. I said she was welcome to be with us and we waited and encouraged each other. He is coming, I told them; he will not desert us.

"How will he come?" "In what form?" "What is the baptism by fire he and John spoke of?"

And many questions were asked and few answers were given except to have faith and be patient. So, we ate and sang and prayed as we had learned, going out for a while and returning to the room situated just outside the walls of Jerusalem.

On the fiftieth day it happened. The Spirit descended upon us in the near dark. Those in the room, including the apostles, were infused with the Spirit which came as a wind, although the windows and doors were locked, and it materialized as small candle flames. Once one was touched, they had the power to speak diverse languages that no one understood in the room. But the real flame was lit inside of us, and from that day the Spirit possessed us and our eyes shone bright and our breath deepened and we felt we were lifted to some pinnacle of existence.

So empowered, we went outside where more disciples had gathered after they had heard the sound from heaven, and were amazed that they could interpret their own language in the words of those baptized by the Spirit, for they had come from near and far for the celebration of Shavuot.

This was the sign that we were to preach the word of our Lord to all nations, and we would go out from there and do just that, inspired. As we all mingled, I remembered the words that Jesus gave me in the dream and stood and, in a voice which I never knew I had, proclaimed that the prophesy of Joel was fulfilled.

And afterward,
 I will pour out my Spirit on all people.
 Your sons and daughters will prophesy,
 your old men will dream dreams,
 your young men will see visions.

And I went on to quote from the Psalms. Everything happened as promised, and I reiterated that Jesus was the way, truth, and light, and anyone who believed in him could be saved. I said that he was the Lord and the Christ and was approved by God, his Father. And yet they had him crucified, but even then they can repent and be forgiven, and many came and were baptized with the Holy Spirit, the internal flame of God which lifted up hearts and gave assurance; and we breathed as we had breathed our first breath as infants, and worried not, and wondered not, but took up the hope of life as a child, full of the air of a pure life, and the fire of the Spirit, without questions or doubts in our minds.

We broke out of the church room and preached around Jerusalem that Jesus had risen; we also prayed customary prayers every day in the temple—I, along with John and his brother James, and James the brother of Jesus, and others.

The community grew over the months; many were converted along with those already baptized. We were surprised how rapidly the word spread, and how people came to us to be cured and receive the Spirit. And people sold their property and put the money in front of us so that no one in the community was destitute. We all helped each other.

People gave as they could, and received as they needed. This charity appealed to many outsiders, as did our kindness, despite having our Master crucified. Our lack of retribution was heeded as well as our love and concern for each other and our mutual decency and respect, which were in vivid contrast to the barbarous and brutal culture of the Romans.

But we still had to proceed warily. Some disciples were open about their conversion; others were secretive and made ways to identify each other with a word or a handshake, for we had heard later of a man called Saul, a Jew and a Pharisee, who was seeking out the Grecian Jews for their lack of respect for the temple, and was persecuting them in Jerusalem. He was terrorizing the baptized communities as well, and I told the people to be wary of him, and not to preach in his presence.

As I was foremost in the Jerusalem congregation, I appointed Mattias as the twelfth apostle, since Judas had fled and had bought land to work with his blood money, as he said, although there were rumors that he had hanged himself. But knowing Judas as I did, I thought that was unlikely, and purchasing the land he had spoken about was more in character.

The twelve of us formed a tight group of confederates, and discussed proceedings and strategies, and outlined our immediate plans for expansion and regional organization.

John and I worked together in Jerusalem and prayed and preached and we met in the temple in Solomon's Colonnade, and the people were receptive as the word of the Lord was continued, and the people were impressed that even after his death, we proceeded with his mission; others were disgusted. And the community grew and some priests and Pharisees were also converted. No one was immune, or refused.

18

THE ROAD TO DAMASCUS

IT WAS WHEN, ON THE WAY to the Beautiful Gate of the temple, a lame man was carried and laid down, as he was every day. He then begged for alms. I went to him and asked him to look at me, which he did, imploringly. "I cannot give you money, but your legs I will return to you in the name of Jesus of Nazareth." With that I held him and raised him and he stood unsteadily, then let go of my hand as his legs and feet resumed some power.

I held his hand and he walked with us to the temple. And I spoke to those gathered as they wondered at my power, but they had crucified the one whose power I invoked. And the words we spoke from the Scriptures amazed them also: how could unlettered men speak like this of Moses and Samuel and the prophets? We, of course, had learned from Jesus. And many were baptized when they heard and saw this.

The Sanhedrin were incensed, and some disciples were duly arrested. Annas the high priest and Caiaphas were there, frustrated at our outspokenness and at the continuity of the preaching even after Jesus was executed, but were restrained when we said we were no threat to either Rome or Judaism.

In the morning, they questioned us again, but I was able to speak the truth clearly that only through Jesus of Nazareth, the one they crucified, could a man be made whole or be saved. They had worried because killing Jesus did not seem to reduce his influence, for it was self-generating. They knew this and warned us not to continue. But I said we pay heed to God, not man. And they reluctantly let us go, not wanting to cause any further trouble amongst the people, whose mood had turned slightly in our favor.

We preformed healing where we could in the name of Jesus, and preached repentance, for the coming was near, perhaps any day, and this incited people to act. Barnabas sold his property and placed it at the community's disposal, and others as well, including Ananias and Sapphira. These two were dishonest before men and God, not disclosing the full amount of their sale. Of course, what they gave was up to them, but to pretend to give all while keeping some back amounted to theft and dishonesty, and the Lord, not I, dealt the punishment to them, which frightened us all with its immediacy and severity.

But then we heard that one of our disciples and servers of the community, Stephen, was arrested by Saul who was back in Jerusalem, and was sent before the authorities. After he was tried, Stephen was stoned to death under the watch of Saul, and the disciples were frightened and hid, and became more secretive.

It was said Saul targeted the baptized Grecian Jews rather than the orthodox Jews because of their attitude to the law. James and I discussed Stephen with others, and it seemed that he had angered the Sanhedrin and Saul by his outspoken opposition to the temple cult in Jerusalem.

"Why did he speak out like that?" I asked. "It's not our belief that the temple is idolatry. It's the opposite."

John said he knew him, and he was a zealot who had, like Jesus, strict views about the law and how it should be kept, and that the Mosaic religion had to be restored to what it was before it was contaminated by the Sadducees and other Grecians. "It was what Jesus preached, after all," he said.

As I believe, Stephen foresaw an essentially Jewish following of Jesus—and a return to a purer Mosaic law. What did it mean for the future of our mixed community? Not all shared a common vision, as was evident. Stephen was brazen and outspoken and talked fearlessly of his vision of the Son of Man. I warned James and John about speaking out with too much zeal, but they rebuked me for my timidity. I said no, not that, but we have a commission and we can't fulfill it if we are all dead, and to exercise caution, as Jesus said.

Saul continued that year to persecute the faithful and severely retarded the growth of the community. After he left Jerusalem, he headed towards Damascus and there was some temporary relief in Jerusalem, but we were hunted by his associates.

But then the most amazing event occurred. News about Saul's conversion arrived. He had a vision and saw and heard the Lord. From that moment Saul was freed and proclaimed the risen Christ as the Messiah. Nothing was impossible for God, but many disciples were skeptical; others kept quiet about it, since it was Saul, the persecutor. It was hard to believe— Saul? The executioner of Stephen? The Grecian Jew, trained Pharisee, turning under a vision from Jesus?

I asked for details but they were not known. Only that he was knocked off his horse, went into a trance, and awoke as a disciple of Christ, blinded. I still found this incredible and would pray on it for it had many implications—Saul was influential. However, nothing was heard of him for three years after that. It was said he went to Damascus and thence to Arabia. But I was thankful, if it were true, to have Palestine freed from his terror, and it was proof that the Lord was with us, as promised.

I, myself, kept an open opinion. Was Saul set up by the authorities to infiltrate the new community, as some said? What did he know about the works and words of Jesus and the promise of salvation? What did he know of Jesus' words and parables? Some said he was an imposter, posing as a follower. I wanted to know more about him and his conversion, but soon, his actions spoke loudly to us. But why the Lord had gifted him, of all people, left us guessing.

I then remembered the words of our Lord to me: that what he did, whom he chose, whom he sent, was none of my business.

In the following three years the message of salvation was preached throughout Judea, Samaria, Galilee, Syria and Damascus, Cyprus and Cyrene and Antioch, headed by the apostles. The spreading of the word was largely undertaken by the diaspora disciples who had fled Jerusalem during the persecution.

Then, three years after his conversion, Saul came to Jerusalem. He had been preaching in the synagogues in Damascus and was threatened by the Jews there. There was an oral tradition about Jesus already spreading, and he, Saul, could have learned of many sayings and doings of Jesus from testimonies and from those he had persecuted. He thence came to Jerusalem, supposedly to seek me out. During his absence, the Jerusalem congregation had multiplied again.

He arrived on a wet and muddy day. He was welcomed by Barnabas into the house prepared for him, away from the others. James, brother of the Lord, and myself met him, and he was warmed and fed. He was a well-presented man; even after all his travels he looked clean, tidy, with shortish black hair and neat beard. He dressed sufficiently well in comparison to us, and carried the air of a sturdy man, a man of intelligence and insight, and conviction.

He was alert and active, and even when he smiled, he looked serious. He filled the room with his presence, and he was single-minded, and spoke directly with a fixed gaze.

We ate and drank and listened to his journeys. He told us of his time in Arabia when he pondered his future after his conversion and his baptism by Ananias of Damascus. All in all, he was a man larger than life—precise, lettered, and forthright. He told us how he preached immediately in the synagogues after his conversion, but said his real mission was to the gentiles, and he had already done so to the God-fearers in Damascus and Tarsus.

After he had rested, I quietly sat with him, and James sat with us but apart, but in no way was he intimidated. Saul insisted on calling me Cephas as he had heard the name was originally given to me by the Lord. I did not object; it meant the same as Peter. I asked him if he could describe his conversion on the road to Damascus. He was reluctant. "It is between the Christ and myself; I do not want to describe what happened. And I do not want to seem to be boastful." But he could see we were a little taken aback, expecting something more from him.

"My gospel will be the gospel for the gentiles," he said, forthrightly. He seemed convinced of that. James and I took notice, for preaching to the gentiles had arisen amongst us without resolution, but Saul had proclaimed his own gospel.

"Your gospel?" I asked. "Then how should we understand your gospel, Saul, as there can only be one?"

"I agree," he said. "So, I come in humility to proclaim one gospel to all men, but all men are not one to begin with." We balked at his words but did not interfere, as we were prepared to listen.

"I had no doubts that my persecution of the baptized was correct, and I pursued it with zeal. I was not afraid or remorseful. I had never had hallucinations or wild dreams before; in every way I considered myself balanced and reasonable. Those with me told me I was suddenly flung off my horse and I saw Jesus standing before me, as you must have seen him after his resurrection, and he spoke to me directly."

He paused and was reflective. I asked him, "What was he like?"

"Just as you had seen him," he replied.

We waited but he did not add anything. "His grace filled me," he continued. "I could feel it enter my body, flowing through me completely with power and heat. For he opened my eyes to the disgrace of my persecutions, and my disbelief in all things related to him, but then I was given knowledge not passed on to mortals. I was to have full participation in the preaching of his word and had no need of worldly instruction. And for three days I was blind."

With that, tears came to his eyes. "I was wrongly born, not of the right time, but I am still one of you—one of the twelve, an apostle, as Christ has approached me directly and appeared to me and instilled me with the Spirit for my mission."

"Did he speak directly to you?" I asked.

"Yes, and the others heard a sound and saw a light but distinguished nothing. He asked me calmly why I was persecuting him, and he said to go to Damascus and to be instructed what to do there. I was baptized and started preaching and was threatened by the Jews and came here to Jerusalem to seek the first of the apostles, Cephas, himself."

I held my beard. "What do you preach?" I asked.

"That Jesus is the Christ, the Savior, the Son of God. That he died for our sins, and we are saved by his death and resurrection. These things were given directly to me, not by any teaching of man. It was revealed to me graciously by the Lord Jesus Christ to be delivered to the gentiles, who, like me, require a free conscience, full participation, and full faith in salvation."

"Do you preach to the Gentile God-fearers, or the pagans?" I asked. He said to the God-fearers, but the day will come when the pagans will also be opened to the truth.

"We are not in any disagreement, Saul. You will continue to preach as you please, as revealed to you, and we will not hamper you."

I looked to James and he nodded, but solemnly, for there were still doubts about this man who not so long ago had run from door to door dragging Christians out of their homes and into prison. We kept the whereabouts of others secret and told him to remain hidden as much as possible while he was with us. We let him rest, and asked no more questions then.

Outside, I spoke to John, who had joined us, and James. "We must take what he says at face value. We cannot deny, accuse, or protest. We will see what fruits he produces. But keep him at arm's length and divulge nothing of our community, yet. We will learn about him and his preaching in time."

James remained unsure as he could not describe the Lord, and such a sudden change of heart from bitter cold to spiritual heat was questionable. But the persecution of the baptized in Jerusalem had ceased by then thanks to Saul's conversion, and James was reminded of our own sudden calling and acceptance.

We asked Saul to remain hidden but he started to go out talking to some Jewish leaders and preaching to a small number of Grecian Jews. I would have liked to hear what he said, and I made a clandestine visit to the synagogue when, during a talk, Saul suddenly became transfixed, shaking and writhing on the floor, his eyes open but blind to everyone. I went to him. "Saul, Saul, wake up." He stopped shaking, and with eyes wide open, sat up mumbling incoherently. I asked him what he had seen but he did not reply and I took him out of the synagogue and back to his home where he slept.

That night I told James and he said he, Saul, must leave, immediately. He had attracted too much attention and the authorities saw him as a traitor. Saul told us after he rested that Jesus had commanded him to preach to the gentiles again in his trance. So, the next day he seemed fully recovered and, on our advice, he agreed to return to Tarsus.

And so, undercover, he made his escape, but first shook our hands and hoped we could cooperate in our teaching always. And for many years we did not hear from him except by word of mouth that he was successfully preaching in Syria and Cilicia.

19

SIMON MAGUS

BUT WE STILL HEARD NEWS of things that did concern us. Saul's success among the gentiles was growing and could not be ignored. What was vital to our mission was unity. But Saul seemed to have his own direction, and his interpretation of the sacred word was increasingly under scrutiny.

Even so, the commission given to us by Jesus was fully undertaken. Philip successfully baptized many thousands in Samaria, but he reported there was, disappointingly, no reception of the Spirit. John and I left Jerusalem and went to Samaria to intercede. We were pleased with what Philip had done, and the community was large but somewhat lacking, and John and I administered the Holy Spirit by laying on our hands, and they received the Spirit enthusiastically, and the community was forged and prospered. And thereafter Philip regained the power.

At that time there was a godlike pretender preaching in Samaria; his name was Simon Magus. His reputation for magical acts such as levitation and other illusions preceded him, but he was baptized by Philip, and remained with him. Simon was fascinated by the way I could affect people, strangers he had never met, with the laying on of hands. After we arrived, Simon came to us one night in our lodgings and asked to speak with us. I agreed, but John resisted, and left.

Simon was a small man, rotund, long hair and dressed ornately. It was said he could do wonders even before his baptism, and we had a mutual interest. We sat and drank wine and finally, he said, "I have seen the things that Philip and you can do. But I can't see how it's done." I told him it was the power of faith. He looked surprised. "That's all?"

I said the power was bestowed by another, not of this world. He replied, "Yes, he was crucified and rose from the dead, as Philip taught us, and went to heaven. His miracles are well known already. But Philip can still perform them if he is not here?"

Then he sucked in air through his nostrils and removed his head covering. "I want to buy into this power." I asked him what he meant. "I will pay if you give me the power of the hands. The healing I can do, but the hands is something I don't understand."

"It is to be bought with love and belief in the Messiah, not with money."

"But you see, I know your tricks, and I can do most of them, but this power to make strangers collapse and cry and writhe and proclaim in unknown languages, how is it done? I have never before seen this performed. I would have thought it was prearranged but I have experienced it personally. Is a herb or root administered firstly?"

"I have told you."

"Come Peter, we are men of the world; I know how Jesus performed his miracles, and I can tell you."

I was interested in what he had to say because of his repute as a magician. I said, "The miracles were not tricks or magic, and you know a lot; is it from hearsay?"

"I have eyes and ears everywhere, Peter. All magic is play, illusion; people are gullible, and you know it. From the first time I heard about Jesus I was in awe; he was the best."

"You are deluded if you think he was a magician, or merely a faith healer. He came with the power of God."

"Perhaps, but I am a practical man, and I know how these things are done." He held up some fingers and asked, "How many fingers am I holding?" I could not answer. My sight was not so sharp, and getting worse. "See," he said. "Our eyes weary as we age; despite that, people always believe what they see and hear."

"Explain his miracles then," I said.

"It's done the same way I do my magic. No man works alone. You set the stage and determine what people see. You control events through preparation. I know he has the twelve, but within the disciples there is an inner circle of trusted assistants, maybe only two or three, well paid, and no one knows who they are."

"How do they work?"

"They prepare the way with money. Your community is very wealthy, I know it. Every day the people give you money. I know about Barnabas and the others. And when Ananias and Sapphira sold their land, you cursed them to death for holding more back than they needed. Judas put his hand in the bag and was punished, some say by hanging, but the bag wasn't big enough and it overflowed and the money was invested, and still is, at considerable interest. And more comes every day. The rich want to buy eternal life so they do what is told, sell everything and wait, as you said. So, there was no shortage of finance to assist in setting things up."

He stopped, drank. "I will tell you how I would have done it, and it is the same. His confidants went ahead to a village and made arrangements— prepared a supposedly sick man, or whatever, paid them well to act out a scene. Take the ten lepers. As I recall, they were well away from the disciples and Jesus, because they were unclean. Did anyone really inspect them first? They were probably also covered and were not healed immediately, but were told to present to the priest in the temple. They were never seen again."

"One returned."

"Yes, to show himself as clean—for he was never unclean."

"And Lazarus?" I asked.

"He never died, that was the rumor. Mary and Martha were good friends of Jesus; it was easily prearranged. And the response of Mary and Martha, I am told, was quiet and subdued, and they only worried about the smell. The others, as Jesus said himself, they were only sleeping. And the cripple you cured by the Beautiful Gate, he was a long-term beggar, it was his livelihood, and you took him from it, so he could never beg again. When you cured him, he had little trouble standing with your help. Does it make you wonder?"

"Jesus fed thousands with a few fish and loaves."

"But you did not see the baskets of fish and loaves brought behind the crowd and passed to the front."

"But there were others who were healed after a testimony of the people that they had been crippled or invalid for years."

"And who was counting? The invalid was partially crippled, and with the power of money he managed to walk."

"I saw Jesus walk on water."

"Did you? He walked on sunken rocks. Everything can be explained. The real deception was in keeping it all a secret from the rest of you."

"He quelled storms and waves."

"He quelled your fear of the storms; they remained the same."

"You don't worry me, magician. He made our boats full of fish when there were none in the sea."

"He knew what time the fish would be plentiful, and where, because the fish were restrained and then released by his accomplices. But this laying on of hands, I have never seen it. How is it done? I want that power and will pay."

"You will never see the day, Simon Magus."

"They think I can fly, Peter. Why not come to Rome where I will do a demonstration in the Forum? They treat me like a god."

"The only way you can receive the Spirit is to repent and believe in the risen Lord."

"Risen? You really believe that? That was an outstanding illusion. I have two theories, Peter, as it is recorded, and well for you to listen. Jesus was switched at the garden of Gethsemane when you all slept (it's well known you did sleep). Herod sent one to replace Jesus, a Zealot, already condemned, in return for a payment to his family. Herod was also well paid and he did not condemn Jesus. And the Zealot spoke from the cross strange words, I am told. In the dark at Gethsemane no one noticed, but it was up to Judas to identify him, as it had been prepared. At the tomb the guards were bribed, opened the tomb, cut the body into pieces and spread them around the land, and Jesus was there the next day, radiant.

"But my second theory is also possible. Jesus was crucified and died and was buried and the body again taken out, for payment, and cut into pieces and spread over the land, and the switch with another was made at the tomb. I was told witnesses had trouble recognizing Jesus after he had risen. It was because it wasn't him, brother, but another like him, and he spoke little and was gone quickly."

"He came and went like a ghost; we saw him many times in Jerusalem," I said, undisturbed.

"He never left the room, Peter. There was a secret place, hidden, where he or another stayed, until he appeared and disappeared, known only to his accomplices who made wind and the sounds that frightened everyone and lit the candles you thought were flames of the Spirit. And he said very little. And now he is gone to who knows where, living a complacent life. He has been seen with that Mary of Magdala."

"Simon, you make a mockery of everything but I tell you your day is near and you will meet the Lord and be shaken and broken and cut and left to die, because your mockery has been heard, and it will not be repealed. You know nothing of the Spirit—only how to cheat and lie and deceive people."

With that I stood to leave him. Before I left, he said, "Do not say those things, Simon Peter. I beg you, retract them."

"So now you believe? Are you any different to a demon?"

I knew he was false because of the power I myself had in healing given by the Lord. And I had lived side by side with him. I could see how many would test our faith now and in the future.

But my mission was also to build up and fortify the baptized in Judea and Galilee, and they were spreading at an incredible pace. People came in their hundreds to be baptized and the disciples were weary but worked every day and the communities grew and needed organization and direction. But many converts spoke of things that had never happened or in exaggerated terms, and they were warned to only report what had actually occurred, and so they discussed and prayed, waiting for the final hours to come.

Makeshift community rooms were rented and put up but even they could not hold the people, and so small edifices were constructed in towns with the specific purpose of prayer and meetings.

I continued to do my work advising, preaching, and healing. On one occasion I was brought to a bedridden man in Lydda called Aeneas who had been stricken for eight years without walking. I remembered the words of Simon Magus and I did not contest this man's story but felt his legs and applied pressure where I thought he responded, and felt the lumps which I smoothed out, and I told him in the name of Jesus to be healed. And he slowly rose, putting his feet on the ground, and I held his hand and he stood, and we walked slowly outside where people waited, and they were overcome, for he hobbled along, stronger with each step.

I asked one man if it had been eight years since he was able to walk. He replied, "Many years, Peter." Not only were they impressed but they were baptized in the name of our Lord.

I felt the power flow from my hands into his legs. I knew the power was from the Lord, but I felt it stronger each time as each time my faith increased, as it needed to be, because the same day word came from the disciples in Joppa that a good woman follower had died.

I went with them on a short journey to find her in bed in an upper room; she looked to be sleeping, and I asked the women there to leave the room. When alone, I felt her forehead and she was still warm. I whispered her name, "Tabitha," and then knelt and prayed solemnly for some time while massaging her feet. I looked at her and thought I saw a movement of her little finger. I then said, "Tabitha, rise up." And she opened her eyes and slowly sat up.

I took her hand and we went outside, and the people laughed and cried for they said she had died but now lived. Again, I saw the magician's face and heard his voice and had to pray hard to keep him away. When outside, I asked the people, "Who said she had died?"

There was a discussion and one woman spoke up and said she had proclaimed it. I went to her and held her hand and she was cold. "How do you know these things?"

"I was a doctor in my hometown," she said. "I worked in Joppa many years. They called for me to come here." With that I let her be, and went to stay with one Simon the tanner, who had invited me to his home.

20

GENTILES AND JEWS

SIMON THE TANNER WAS AN INTERESTING MAN, a God-fearer, who was kept well informed by the passing pilgrims. Simon then asked me by what power I could raise the dead. I told him Tabitha was not raised but raised herself after I had prayed to the Lord over her, and as her spirit had not left, Jesus gave her the strength, for she had been a good and holy woman.

I told him I knew of many who doubted the power but I could only tell him what took place. He said why not bring back the many to life? Why just the few, for many were good and holy? And I said one day it would happen. I did not know why Jesus chose a few for the ordeal here and now, but it was a sign, surely, that the dead will rise soon, and he would come as judge of all.

He looked pale and wan, and asked for the Spirit, and I lay my hands on him and he awoke and his eyes were bloodshot and his face sustained a renewal, and he was released and instilled at that moment.

And in the evening as I slept a strange dream of animals being lowered on a sheet came to me—all animals such as sheep, goats, pigs, rabbits, calves, lambs, fowl, birds—mild and supine, and no animal was greater than another, or cleaner. When the sheet was lowered, I distinctly heard a voice in my head. "Eat, for they are clean." I said, "No, some are forbidden." But the voice said, "What God has made, let no man call unclean." I woke, but could not understand. I put it aside because I had no dealing with husbandry and wondered why this animal dream came to me until a disturbance outside aroused me.

The disciples had also made their lodgings in the town, and were drawn out to an alarm, and people came to me saying that I was summoned to Caesarea by a centurion called Cornelius. This man was a God-fearer and gave generously to the poor and the synagogue.

"What did he want?"

"Come and see, he is asking for you."

Because of his position and admiration by the people I said I would go with some of my disciples, and we set out and were accompanied by Cornelius' men. When we reached Caesarea, Cornelius came to me and bent on his knee. I told him to stand and he said he was asked to send for me in a vision. I then explained to him that Jesus had risen, and we were to save the faithful, and Cornelius had proven himself in faith. At that moment Cornelius received the Holy Spirit, and he spoke freely in tongues, and I understood the dream I had, for everyone was to be admitted into the kingdom who believed under the new covenant.

It was plain to me then. But the people around were astounded that a Gentile should receive the Holy Spirit, as well as his followers. But there it was. A non-Jew had been converted to the Lord and I could only praise God for his mercy, as all men were to be open to the word, and on hearing should receive the Spirit. I could not explain it to the people then; only by my actions could I show what could be done, and Cornelius was duly baptized with water, and I was taken into his house to eat with them.

The disciples told me Cornelius identified God with Caelus, and was a pagan. Others said he prayed to God and was a God-fearer. I said if any man is open to truth and accepting, he shall not be denied.

But it shocked many when they heard of the baptism, and they continued to criticize me as we walked out of the town. Cornelius was uncircumcised and did not follow the law of Moses. I could see it as a possible stumbling block on the path to a universal conversion. I could see how Judaism should be changed in customs and beliefs, but at the same time assuring the Jews nothing had changed, except belief in the Lord Jesus. The new covenant was a rock on which many would stumble, but many would also find refuge.

When we arrived back in Jerusalem word of this event had preceded us. There was disunity and antagonism had been aroused by my conversion of Cornelius and having entered his house and supped with the gentiles there. The brothers John and James both asked for an explanation. I said we needed to discuss this, and that evening after prayer and dinner, the apostles met. I had to explain the dream I had about the animals gathered together and the words "What God made clean no man should make unclean."

"It was a dream, Peter. Did you see the Lord? Did he speak to you?" John asked.

"No, but it was prophetic, and the next day I had a summons from Cornelius as it had been instructed to him in a dream also. And didn't Jesus chide the Pharisees for their strict adherence to the law?"

John said that the elders could justify it temporarily in relation to the dream, and then said, "Jesus only preached to Jews, and never to gentiles. He said salvation is from Israel."

"Then what to make of his command to preach to all nations?" I asked.

"All nations where there are Jews living," he replied. "Salvation is for the Jews and comes from the Jews." I did not know the Scriptures well enough but I knew Jesus had included gentiles in his scheme of the new earth. But John said, "The messianic age is the end of days when all will bow down before the one true God and Israel will be restored. We cannot dilute the Scriptures."

I said I was in no opposition, but did not understand why it was so controversial. I had blessed a God-fearer. Then they gathered their cloaks around their arms and heads and departed.

There was a fair proportion of the baptized in Jerusalem who would not let go of the Mosaic law and insisted it should be kept by all who professed Jesus, as both the love and forgiveness of Jesus and the law of Moses were necessary for salvation. These were the Pharisees, mainly, who had been converted, the nationalists, the purists, the zealots who had to be accommodated, and they were listened to.

At that time the faithful were not ready to dispense with the Mosaic law and their ceremonies; it was too ingrained and embedded in their culture, as it was in mine, but I had opened myself to the commission of our Lord, to take the word to Jew and non-Jew alike, but was unsure if that should include pagans. But I could see it would have to be handled carefully, for the repercussion could cause serious conflict in the community, which I wanted to avoid at all costs.

I agreed to the proposition that the law be maintained for Jews, but if it was necessary for gentiles was still an open question. The law forbade contact between Jew and Gentile. How was the community to be enabled if this law were kept? Not living and eating together would lead to a schism and division of the brethren, and also the community. It was an issue that had to be dealt with. For to maintain that gentiles had to practice Jewish law, such as circumcision, was closing the door in their face, or alternatively, in the face of the Jews.

The apostles in Jerusalem were divided but sided mainly with keeping the law—certainly for Jews, or even just admitting Jews to the full congregation, and gentiles as proselytes, as it was already. I asked James, Jesus' brother, what he thought. He agreed that presently only Jews should be admitted so that we could keep control over developments. The faith was already spreading to Gentile God-fearers by the work of Saul in Syria and Cilicia and Philip in Samaria. Allowing Samaritans was one thing, but gentiles, with full membership and without circumcision and in avoidance of the law, was something else.

Andrew and James, the brother of John, and I, kept our reservations to see how the Lord would direct us in future. But one certainty I had was that the disciples and leaders were turning to James, the brother of Jesus, for confirmation and affirmation. The conversion of Cornelius had changed their thinking, and increasingly I felt James was sought for leadership over my own. He was more centered on the law than I, and more of an adherent, and trust and agreement in Jerusalem was skewing from my own authority to his.

Then, after years of almost trouble-free preaching and growth of the baptized community in Jerusalem, Herod Agrippa I took on himself a resurgence of persecution. The conversions were probably too successful for his liking and, as he was always in the need of approval, he began to attack us once again. It was said he was jealous of the preachers who were gathering contributions which should have gone to the temple coffers, and the Jesus haters supported him.

As a result, James the elder, brother of John, son of Zebedee, was taken off the streets preaching, and arrested. James was a foundation stone of the community but an outspoken, fiery tempered man, who was emboldened with the missionary zeal and the righteous word. He could barely be restrained when he preached in his thunderous voice, and he was quickly executed by the sword under orders of Herod.

I went to John, his younger brother, and he cried. "Why did they do that? James was a good man, a good adherent and caused no trouble. They wanted Saul, or you," he said. I said James would be rewarded, as promised, as from the first days he was with us, always at the Lord's side, always boisterous in his proclamations; one could only admire his spirit. He never doubted the Lord; he was as good and faithful a servant as there could be. And his selflessness and humility were an example for us all.

"I will miss him," he said simply, for John was also great in his adherence and faith, solid and manifestly subservient to the Lord, as well a charismatic apostle and brother. It was, as I realized, the fate that awaited us all. And so, time was precious, for the days were dwindling.

We went about our business, trying not to draw attention from the authorities, but Herod could see that executing James had pleased many of the Jews and priests, and then, before I could plan anything in way of escape, soldiers put their hands on me, and in the name of King Herod arrested me, and took me to prison.

Some saw this, and went to tell the others. From that moment it was like looking through a veil. The arrest and the image of Herod and the imprisonment were as if I was watching events from above, out of my body. They followed a warped, dreamlike sequence; voices were distorted and people seemed ghostly, like figments. I had no feelings, no fear, and was told I would be tried in the morning.

I rested in jail, chained at both hands, but neither in fatigue or in pain, I simply rested. There were many guards and they drank and ate and took turns to sleep, which I did also, but without food or drink, but I cared less.

As I slept, someone loosened my chains and a voice said to follow. The figure was completely covered from head to foot but was tall and imposing. Who was it? The figure took me past the guards who were all sleeping in contorted positions to the outside, and left me.

In the street I realized it was not a dream and, suddenly, I saw where I was and went directly to the house of Mary, John Marks' mother. I knocked on the door and a servant girl recognized my voice, and she was stunned and ran to tell the others. Mary came and let me in, and we embraced.

She took me to another room where John Mark and some disciples were gathered praying to the Lord and said I would be safe there, but to remain silent. She brought me soup and some food and drink and I rested for the evening, unable to explain anything. The next morning John Mark came to me and we sat and talked. I told him my story and he was pleased, but I had to remain quiet until the authorities were convinced that I had left Jerusalem. He told me many had already left and were heading for Cyrene, Cyprus, and Antioch where others had previously gone.

John Mark was a friend, and we had known each other for a long time, in fact years. He was a disciple and a keen servant of the Lord. His mother

Mary was a gentle, holy woman who worshiped the Lord and opened her house as a prayer house. John Mark was a dedicated man but difficult to reconcile with. I could not get close to him and he rarely spoke his thoughts. He was better educated than most of us and could write basic Greek and Aramaic, but imperfectly, it was said. He was a keen official and managed the tasks assigned to him well. He was not a preacher by nature, but his sincerity and willingness to serve were very useful to the cause, especially when it came to coordinating and communicating with the various towns.

He told me it was not safe in the house and he would arrange for me to take cover in another place. I went into hiding and knew that James, the Lord's brother, could lead and inspire the community in my absence. It was as if men and women were ripe since Jesus' death for the words that fell on them, and identified as brothers and sisters. And more came every day. They longed for salvation, the time of the Messiah, which we proclaimed as having arrived.

I kept in touch with some of the apostles as they visited me in the safe house until pressure was released with the death of Herod. This was totally unexpected and we could not but feel relieved. Now that Herod was gone, I came out of hiding and again associated with the disciples, and gradually revealed myself freely in the open.

21

SAUL RETURNS TO JERUSALEM

ONE DAY, BARNABAS TOLD ME that Saul was coming to Jerusalem after five years since his first visit. He had sent word to Barnabas that he wanted to present himself to the disciples and for recognition of his work, and would stay with Barnabas. Saul and Barnabas were already acquainted from their synagogue days under the teacher Gamaliel but Barnabas did not go into any details. Apparently, they communicated by letter and advised and encouraged each other.

Saul's success in Damascus and Tarsus and his approaching visit reopened the debate on converted gentiles. It was no longer possible to delay the issue. In Antioch, the number of followers were growing every day due to the diaspora Jews, now baptized in Christ, and it was apparent that someone from Jerusalem would have to coordinate and regulate affairs there sometime soon. It was also said that the Gentile numbers in Antioch were contesting that of the Jews. Many converted Jews, originally from Cyrene and Cyprus, left Jerusalem for Antioch to avoid persecution after Stephen's execution, and they preached to Grecian Jews there.

It was mooted that I might go there to regulate proceedings as I was unofficially proclaimed missionary to the gentiles. It wasn't a title I vaunted. It was my interpretation of the words of the Lord, but I did not want to separate myself from the apostles who were increasingly behind James. I did not put myself forward, and as events unfolded, the task fell onto another after Saul's visit.

And so, on a seemingly normal day in Jerusalem in the summer, Saul came again and was met by Barnabas who took him in. Saul immediately associated with the apostles who were gathered in the Cenacle and they were cordial, unlike the first visit when they shunned and refused to sanction his visit or his works. This time was different, entirely, and before two days the issue arose concerning the law and Saul's teaching. It was mainly a private affair with some of the apostles and elders present, with James and I attending.

Firstly, the apostles recognized his work in Syria, particularly Damascus. In fact, he had worked tirelessly converting the God-fearing gentiles, who proclaimed the Jewish God and accepted Jesus as his Son, and were baptized in his name. But the time had come, he said, when his work, that is, his teachings in Damascus and Tarsus and Cilia, should be officially recognized as the same as that in Jerusalem. This would acknowledge that the gospel he preached was in accord with that of the apostles, and the status of his converts equal to those in Jerusalem.

Seeing that he had taken on this task of recognition himself was admirable, as he was not called to Jerusalem to account. We thought it best for Saul to explain his gospel and for us then to consider it. Saul said his preaching to the gentiles had been very successful but had met with serious opposition from the converted Jews. He said he was ordained by God to preach to the gentiles as his ordination had come from visions and direct contact with Jesus. And what he preached was salvation through faith in the death and resurrection of Jesus Christ. As it was written, the just will gain life through faith—that Christ died for our sins, that he was crucified, and was resurrected, which accorded with the Scriptures. And after that he appeared to Cephas and to all the apostles, and to five hundred others on the Mount of Olives.

I looked to James, and he seriously studied Saul, and made no remark or gesture regarding the five hundred. James asked him directly, "Do you teach Jesus as the Son of God?"

He answered not only as the Son of God, but truly divine. "And I believe, also, in a new covenant with God as revealed by Jesus. Under the old covenant no man was justified solely on the basis of the law; under the new all were justified through faith in Jesus Christ. And I am an Apostle of the Lord. I preach that the letter of the law is not life but death, and this new covenant with God must be accepted to gain eternal life—as the new recognition demands, and assures us."

I was surprised how adamant Saul was on this point. He at once referred to another revelation that he had in which he was elevated to the third heaven and saw things and was told things no man should see or hear; he said only that the Father and Son were seated on thrones in heaven and the gates were of circling flames of fire, and the streets as if paved with gold. Such beauty, he said, was truth incarnate. That revelation had led him to come to Jerusalem to seek recognition for his work, which originated in the command and ascent of the Lord.

We listened intently and gazed at each other. Should a man be given such a vision? It was akin to the transfiguration, but beyond that, even.

James spoke and said his work was fruitful, and we were not to interfere, but some agreement must be reached regarding the law, since Saul had encountered such fierce opposition from the baptized Jews. It was then that some of the disciple elders and even some of the apostles gently questioned Saul regarding the law. They were just as adamant that the law had to be kept for complete salvation, at least some of them. They reiterated that Jesus had accepted the law in spirit, if not to the letter.

They argued that Saul had not access to the life and works and teachings of Jesus and that he was proposing himself as an Apostle. With that Saul was visibly incensed. But James interceded and was willing to accept the truth of his teaching and said that gentiles, that is, the God-fearing gentiles, need not be circumcised; it was only necessary for Jews—as it was not presently required for the Jewish proselytes under the law, for the law had not been abolished, nor would it be.

His preaching on salvation and the divinity of Jesus were acceptable, but saying that Jesus was God was not in agreement. And it was agreed that Saul should emphasize more the obedience and servitude of discipleship, as well as the humility, kindness, and balm of the love of Jesus. Faith was essential, but as a result, the way the disciples conducted themselves should reflect the life of Jesus, for as he said, the way was difficult and strewn with thorns and shale, and no one could tread easily.

In consequence, Saul was reminded to remember the poor always, as a cornerstone of adherence to the teachings of the Lord. Saul seemed a little quizzical, but adjourned discussion, as approval had been largely assented to. As a result, Saul came in and out and went and preached in the temple for the following weeks and was unto himself until we learned of a plot by the Grecian Jews, whom he once worked with, to kill him, and we secreted him out of Jerusalem back to Tarsus with the help of some disciples.

James and Andrew and I walked together and talked about Saul at supper after he was gone. We broke bread and drank wine in remembrance as Jesus asked us to do, and James asked what I foresaw for our community. He said in such a short time it had brought in people from many nations already. But James balked at accepting gentiles fully outside the law. Saul wasn't an Apostle so he did not hear everything Jesus had said and done, but I was sure it was Jesus' intention for all people to hear the word and be saved. I never strayed from that belief. But to preserve unity within the community and congregation was also essential. We had to retain cohesion.

John commented that salvation by faith was acceptable as most of the miracles of Jesus referred to the faith of those cured as having saved them, but the belief that faith was a gift given irrespective of deserving it was a problem. In the case of Saul, he was undeserving, but the gift was still bestowed. Did the gift of faith come before or after baptism? Those that Jesus healed proved themselves worthy through their faith, which preceded the curing.

I agreed that we were saved through our faith, but pointed out that the gift can be accepted or rejected. The gift is on offer to everyone. And I reminded him that not everyone who acknowledges Jesus as Lord will be accepted in the kingdom, so that being a follower denotes a life of discipleship, which was, in action, reminiscent of the Lord's life and teaching.

James took in a deep breath. His eyes looked tired and his face was marked with worry. He was more concerned about preaching to the gentiles. He said the God-fearing gentiles were acceptable, but what of the pagans? "Really, Peter. You think the Greeks and Romans will desert their gods and temples and adopt ours? Continuity of our beliefs, aspirations, worship—that is what must be preserved. The Romans are tolerant but they are dismissive of our Lord and his law. If they do adopt our beliefs, they will bring their own with them. The purity of our own religion and that of the new faith will be polluted with idols and false teachings and superstitious practices, Zeus and Athena, and all the demigods, and the myths they carry with them."

"You are looking too far ahead, James. No one said anything about converting pagans, but if they accept the word of the Lord, we must include them; how can we not? It is said they come to us because of our God, not in spite of him."

"Then what follows will be not what we know now and what we preach, but an adaptation to suit all creeds. Saul, already under the influence of the Greeks, has put faith before everything else. But Jesus never said it was his death that would release people, but the truth and light of the word; his death came at the end."

"But it was fulfilment—the prefect sacrifice," I said. I wanted to point out something to James. "Are we converting the gentiles to Christ or Judaism—or is it the same thing? We already have Gentile God-fearers and they are not required to fully convert as proselytes."

"But if Saul has his way, then it will be, but there must be control from above as to who and what can and cannot be admitted. Where will it end? Greeks should remain Greeks—and for Romans, Persians, Arabians, or Indians to remain as such. Did Jesus really expect all peoples to become Jews? What of our customs, traditions, ceremonies, the law, and the temple? Remember when the customs and beliefs of the gentiles of Persia and Babylon corrupted Israel, and we fell into idolatry?"

"So, on the basis of the past, the pre-messianic past, we deny gentiles their salvation? You know it is written that the gentiles will turn and look to the one true God when the time comes—and it is now."

Andrew later said that Saul may have been more influenced by paganism in Tarsus, where he grew up, than he realized, as he was a Grecian Jew. Why was he so dedicated to the gentiles? Was it because of his visions? Or did he see something redemptive in their philosophy?

James was never fully comfortable with the mission of Saul, and there were others behind him, many in support. "Yes, you, Peter, as apostle to the gentiles, we can accept, but Saul is another thing, entirely."

We walked close to our lodgings and bought some fruit and nuts from a stall. John was still irritable and spoke further. "Saul can't wait to debate with the Greeks on their philosophy, their stoicism, and religion. And with that, their gods. He cannot eliminate them overnight so is it easier to accommodate them? He is moving ahead too quickly."

I said again he didn't talk about preaching to pagans, just gentiles. "But it's the next step, and Saul is well equipped to debate with them. What does the pagan know of the Jewish God and his law, and our culture and traditions and ceremonies, and yet he will be asked to accept it? The Greeks and Romans think we are madmen, but the converts will take what suits them, and disregard the rest. It won't be Judaism and it won't be Christ's community, only in name."

"You have visions, James, but no one can see the future entirely. There are too many trees and Jesus said not to worry about tomorrow, there are enough concerns in one day."

James eased his brow and we went to our homes, wary, but still full of hope, for the promise was being fulfilled and the day and hour were drawing nearer. But my greatest fear was that in our struggle for unity we could enforce an irreparable separation and we didn't fully know what we were walking into. And then, where would the new covenant stand?

22

THE JERUSALEM DONATION

SAUL WAS TO FIGURE AGAIN in the near future. The question of Gentile conversion to the Lord opened again as many converts in Antioch came from the gentiles, and the number of Gentile converts rose, some said alarmingly.

It was almost as if there were two factions emerging within the Christ followers—the Gentile and the Mosaic, emanating in Antioch and reverberating outwards towards Jerusalem. And so, in response, the Jerusalem community decided to send Barnabas to Antioch to head the community there and give it leadership. I said my farewells to Barnabas, but he was under the direction of the Jerusalem congregation headed by James. I simply told him to make sure the Gospel as revealed to us was the same as that preached to the gentiles, and not to take the law too uncompromisingly.

What followed was a wave of conversions, as if all who heard the word were affected and the new covenant was applied to all nations, even the Greeks who populated the city. In spite of this, some of the apostles and elders still saw it as a necessity, and increasingly as a priority, that the God-fearing gentiles become circumcised Jews. Barnabas had decided otherwise in Antioch.

The broader definition proposed by some had definite implications for future directions. It continued as a sore in the side of the Jerusalem community. At this time James had developed fully as a leader. He was respected and admired and his word was carrying more weight as his prominence grew, but we still worked together and supported each other, but the issue of the gentiles was difficult to reconcile at that time, as the baptized Jews in Jerusalem were in the majority and were forceful, and included reformed Pharisees and priests and zealots who saw their religion in terms of a national identity.

The work of Barnabas throughout the year seemed extraordinary; the gentiles responded openly and Barnabas went to Tarsus to ask Saul for help with the preaching, baptisms, and organization of the prayer houses there. Saul agreed, and he also had amazing success in converting the Grecian Jews whom he could reach persuasively, as well as the God-fearing gentiles.

Any doubts we had about Saul were still there but not gaping, and his success was unparalleled, and the prayer house, or simply "church" as they became known, grew rapidly through South Galatia, and the followers of Saul were called "Christians" after Jesus Christ, and Saul's Hebrew name was changed to the Romanized "Paul," probably to disassociate himself from the persecutor, but also to make himself more presentable to the gentiles.

These were significant advances. It brought matters to a head as Judas the Zealot and others, including former Pharisees in Jerusalem, could see that the Jewish nature of the Christian church was being altered, and Jewish membership was being lost in the number of gentiles entering the church, and they insisted in meeting after meeting that gentiles must become Jews to be saved, even as Christians. It was a reversal of what had been decided previously with Paul.

As it was, a great famine spread in Judea at that time. It had been prophesized by Agabus, and Paul and Barnabas were coming to Jerusalem with relief from the church in Antioch the following year. It was much needed and appreciated. It was rumored that the church in Antioch was well provided with money and Paul's ability to bring many wealthy gentiles into the church saw their funds accumulate and distributed to the poor and needy, as it was in Jerusalem, and in fulfillment of their promise. So, they were able to bring a large amount for famine relief.

And word came to me that Paul and Barnabas were coming with bags of coin so I met with them privately and in secret. When Paul and Barnabas entered Jerusalem with a small entourage and deposited the tributes at the door of our house, we talked about the issue of gentiles as an aside. Paul assured me the central message of salvation was always foremost, as was Jesus as the Son of God, and that only through faith in Jesus and his word could men be saved.

He seemed annoyed that I continued that line of questioning from our last meeting.

I inquired why the church in Antioch was so successful. They answered it was the promise of eternal life through Jesus Christ. I asked did the gentiles not argue or resist? He said they were willingly converted into eternal life, but the stumbling block for many was circumcision. As God-fearers they had not needed circumcision, yet as Christians they were being pressured into it by the Jews. It was so disagreeable to them that only the most adamant could go ahead with it.

He said without the need for circumcision the numbers would be far greater than they already were. We agreed on the broad working definitions in the last visit, and did not pursue details, as we thought best for Paul and Barnabas to continue their work, but it would be the vocal adherents on both sides of the Gentile question that would raise the problem to almost a crisis, but there were other things presently at hand.

I had no doubt they would travel again, because I thought that was Paul's intention. In fact, I later learned it was agreed that John Mark would go to Antioch with Paul and Barnabas. And so it was, Paul and Barnabas left Jerusalem together, and I said to Paul to continue the good work, but he replied that the issue of the Gentile Christians and the Jewish Christians should not be emphasized, as they coexisted in harmony, for the present, with respect for the law, and circumcision was not obligatory, but it was still disputable territory. I promised I would go to Antioch to visit them soon, and he told me of his plans for an extensive missionary tour with Barnabas, with the help of John Mark, beginning with Cyprus, and possibly going as far as Pamphylia.

As I said, John Mark was a sturdy character and reliable and could conduct an effective ministry, but working with Paul and Barnabas could inspire conflict. He was only one man, and they two, but the going would also be very difficult in terrain and gospel opposition. So, his services would need to be divided, and I warned John Mark that he must remain his own person, because two great missionaries would both entice his following, and he cannot be divided, and the way would be difficult and testing on all.

But Paul was resolute, as was Barnabas, and John Mark was to accompany them. John Mark was comfortable in Jerusalem and worked from there with ease, at home, with his writing and home duties, unto his own ambitions and endeavors. I did not favor the union.

Paul's zeal won him over. "Let no place remain without hearing the word of the Lord," he said. "Let no man say he knew not, let every head bow at the mention of the Lord's name."

I would see how that turned out, but for now Paul was relentless. He could see the possibility of conversion everywhere, and he would personally take the Lord's word and deliver it, and there were no limits as to what could be achieved. He said once the issue of circumcision was decided favorably, he had plans to build many churches and organize the Gentile communities and extend salvation throughout the empire.

Nothing could stop him. And he said it was an endeavor without end, and would spread the influence of Jesus Christ throughout the world, known and unknown.

I extended to Paul the right hand of friendship and recognition, and he gladly accepted, and they went to Antioch in Pisidia first, and there met with John Mark, and all three set out for Cyprus and beyond.

23

ANTIOCH

I TOLD PAUL I WOULD go to Antioch, and I did the following year while he was on his missionary tour. But further disruptions had emerged among the Jews and the Gentile Christians there. There had been many Grecian Jews from Jerusalem who had descended on Antioch. They tended to be more relaxed with the law, or some might say casual, and the impediment of acceptance of the Mosaic law was overcome by simple avoidance. And Paul and Barnabas had taken up the mantle and taught to the Greek speaking gentiles in Antioch, whom I assumed were God-fearing, and they also favored noncompliance with the law.

When I first arrived, it was obvious that the Jews and converted gentiles were living peacefully together as Christians, but almost like two cultures. And they told me the same thing. They said there was no conflict or feelings of jealousy or even separation. There were Jews who kept the law and the gentiles who were not required to. There seemed to be no dissention or dissatisfaction except that, as we in Jerusalem foresaw, the church was largely being divided into separate factions—Jew and Gentile. I ate and associated freely with the Gentile Christians, although it was forbidden by the law.

In Jerusalem, the problem was somewhat hidden due to the smaller number of gentiles, but Antioch contained a large Gentile segment, and it was growing every day. As the numbers grew, so did the problems. Gentile Christianity was a different complex to Jewish Christianity and the identity of Christianity with Judaism was eroding. What, then, of the Mosaic law? Did it need be kept by Jews and gentiles, Jews only, or neither faction?

The problem, as I saw it, centered on issues of circumcision and eating stipulations. Jews were not to eat with or enter the houses of gentiles. But with the arrival of radical Judaizers from Jerusalem the issue was further fraught by denying gentiles their salvation if they did not keep to the Mosaic law which, among other things, required circumcision. The situation was untenable, and not what had been agreed upon previously with Paul.

Not long after my arrival in Antioch, word of my Gentile association must have gotten back to Jerusalem since an entourage of Judaizers arrived in Antioch shortly afterwards from Jerusalem. They were conservative Jews, some of them ex-Pharisees, nationalists and zealots, who took me aside and spoke to me.

"Peter," said one. "We were disturbed to hear that you were freely eating with the uncircumcised."

I answered, "Why should I not?"

They said, "Because it is forbidden."

"Forbidden? Under the old covenant, but not the new."

"It is the same," they said. "You must cease because many in Jerusalem are concerned by this avoidance of the law."

"And James, did he send you?" I asked.

"No, but he too was in agreement and it came that the law is still the law, and must be upheld by all Christian Jews and gentiles."

Those who had been sent to Antioch were strict observers of the Jewish ceremonial law. The houses of the Jewish faithful were divided from the non-Jewish Christians and they did not eat together. I had no trouble associating with gentiles, eating with them, assisting in any respect. I followed the teachings of Jesus, and saw all men as equal before God.

So, nothing had been resolved since Paul's visit to Jerusalem, except the gentiles did not need to observe the law fully, but the problems were surfacing as the understanding of the undertaking was various. Some of the Judaizers said they were sent by James. But why would James do this unless he was under great pressure? Did he not understand I was here and experiencing firsthand mixed Christianity? Why didn't he trust in me?

With that I had to decide what to do for the best. Paul and Barnabas returned to Antioch presently, and they had heard about the arrival of the Jerusalem Jews and that I had been more reluctant to eat with the gentiles; in fact, I had started to avoid the practice in observance of their sanctions, but I was not happy with it.

I had to decide, and since out last meeting in Jerusalem, whence it was indeed understood that Jews should keep the law, if not the gentiles, I ceased eating with them. It was hard to do since I had made friends, and now I left them because of the impression it made in Jerusalem. I realized that Jerusalem was not Antioch, but it was where the apostles remained, and until some general agreement as to the gentiles and the law was made, I should abide by the majority.

Paul was aghast when he heard this. Barnabas came to me and we talked. They had returned from their missionary work and we were both elated and disappointed. John Mark had left them. I heard that he objected or found it too difficult to preach to the pagans, and was overcome with physical exhaustion as well. He went with Barnabas after he and Paul split for a while, and then left Barnabas and returned to Jerusalem.

Secondly, they heard about my recent refusal to eat with gentiles. "That's the decision from Jerusalem?" Barnabas asked.

"I don't know, but certainly it is the view of an influential group. The zealots want the Jewish identity retained, as I can understand. The new direction of conversion has and will bring such issues up and they will be solved, but for now, I believe we are bound by our own law, until it is no longer deemed necessary."

"When will that be?" he asked.

"I can only suspect soon, for the situation is untenable. The new wave of converts is testimony to that. The protests and anxiety of the gentiles cannot be ignored."

"Then I will follow you, Peter."

I asked him, "Did you quarrel with Paul?"

"We had our differences about John Mark, and other things. It was difficult from beginning to end. Paul will not agree with your decision here."

The issue was even deeper than I expected. When Paul later confronted me in my lodgings, he was uncompromising. He was angered about Barnabas and others having sided with me. After what they had been through together in Lystra and Iconium, and the near death of Paul by stoning by some Jews, he was beside himself with rebuke. I told him when news got back to Jerusalem that I was eating and associating with gentiles, it created a scandal. Perhaps, in time, it can be lifted.

Paul replied, "Were there to be such Christians, not fully Christian, because they were not ceremonial Jews, because they refrained from the Jewish law? Were there to be different levels of Christianity? Were the

God-fearing gentiles saved or not without keeping the law fully? They need certainty in Antioch. It had to be decided or there would be a schism, or, alternatively, the conversion of the Gentile world, in future, would be impossible, and Christianity would remain as a sect of Judaism. Don't you see what's at stake?"

I told him the Gentile God-fearers already lived together but separate, without adopting full conversion. Why can't the Christian gentiles live the same way for now? As non-Jewish Christians? But I knew the number of gentiles in Antioch would soon outnumber Jews there, and in Jerusalem, and everywhere. It was the sheer wight of numbers causing the imbalance. Paul, however, took a more forceful approach.

In a public forum, Paul confronted me again in front of both gentiles and Jews. "Cephas, you, a Jew, have lived like a Gentile. Yet you want gentiles to live like Jews. You are wrong in this matter, and the Gospel of the Lord spells it out for us. It cannot be ignored."

I said I agreed. A decision had to be made. "It has already been made, Cephas, by Jesus Christ himself."

Paul said he wanted to come to Jerusalem again to have the matter resolved for all concerned by the leaders and elders. He said under the guidance of the Holy Spirit, it was achievable. I fully agreed. I had converted the first Gentile, and I was easy eating and communicating with the non-circumcised.

Even though I was in agreement with Paul he was not located in Jerusalem where we had to contend with zealots and ex-Pharisees and nationalists who would never abandon the Mosaic law, even though baptized in the Spirit and by water. Of course, gentiles needed to be converted to the one true God for salvation, but not with trumpeting the victory of Jewish ceremonies and laws over them, but with the guidance of the Holy Spirit.

24

THE JERUSALEM COUNCIL

BACK IN JERUSALEM, PRIVATELY, the adherents confronted me about my position, and I was put under pressure as the Jewish majority held considerable power. James and John were in conditional support, but they too came under the influence of the Judaizers and felt the pressure to adhere to the law. But we tried to keep such divergencies private and not to be confrontational, so that the gentiles could continue with their faith.

As a result, Paul set out for Jerusalem soon after I left, since the gentiles in Antioch were pleading for their full approval as Christians—and their salvation—without adherence to the Jewish law, which in terms of circumcision alone would have kept them outside of salvation.

It was a meeting that I would rather have avoided as it seemed a decision would have to made which would not please everyone. I conferred with many, and opinions were largely that the law should be obligatory, somewhat supported by James. As well, the radicals were asking: why should the Jews carry the burden of the law and the gentiles escape it?

In the beginning, I had not foreseen the problem developing as it had. I rather played it down but now many were causing trouble, as Paul had identified them, but being a Jew, as was Jesus, and an adherent unto the law, I increasingly saw the traditionalist's argument.

What I did not understand is why they inaugurated the debate in the first place. Why should Christianity remain a Jewish sect? If it was to be truly universal, as we all agreed, then each to their own, as long as the gospel was properly taught and practiced for salvation, and the one true God worshiped. The Jewish law was irrelevant, ultimately, but I could not say that aloud.

That's not how the radical Jews saw it. They didn't contradict the Lord Jesus; they just saw it differently and insisted that no one outside the law could be saved, as was our age-old belief, and the belief and practice of Jesus. The one true God was the God of Israel, and all people had to submit to his authority, and to do that completely was to keep the law. The law was the heart of Judaism, and by extension, Christianity. They persistently recalled the sayings of Jesus that the disciples were not to go unto the gentiles.

I believed gentiles could be saved, but I was not the one to preach to them. Paul was a Grecian Jew and, as such, was better qualified to carry the message to the gentiles. So, as I understood it, he had been chosen by God to be the apostle to the gentiles, not I.

I, therefore, at the meeting set my own position that circumcision for God-fearing gentiles was not necessary, as it had never been, and as such, by this example alone, salvation was open to the gentiles without adherence to the Jewish law—that is, they could be fully Christian without becoming fully converted Jews. I quoted sayings from the Lord Jesus that adequately supported the view.

If we allowed Gentile Christians, then they could live as God-fearers living together in harmony but separated from Jews, in fellowship patches, as they did already, such as witnessed in Antioch. However, the sheer number of converts precluded that stance since soon the number of gentiles would outnumber the Jews, and the Jews would be the outsiders, and the weight of opinion must inevitably shift.

The only solution, ultimately, was full community of both Jews and gentiles—full integration, which meant integration outside of the law. But I kept that quiet and thought Paul the best man to present the case, if he so chose.

"But Christian Jews," I maintained, "should follow the law as they saw fit. Secondly, that all Christians should be unified in creed and conviction. This unity would be necessary to withstand current and future opposition. Therefore, being one was essential to the survival of the church."

James was more or less in agreement but stated his opposition again but also in agreement with Paul, but differently oriented. If we allow God-fearing gentiles to become Christians without full conversion to Judaism then we have two-tier Christianity—the Jewish Christians and the Gentile Christians. But I restated to him that that was basically the position already in Judaism with the God-fearers, but they were smaller in number, and it was feasible at the moment, but in the future, it would not be so.

Many opposed this position, but James and John were largely in agreement, somewhat reluctantly, because the general mood was not in accord, but the desire to preserve unity was ultimately paramount. We would see how the Word was to be carried to the nations. But Paul was right: for that to succeed, gentiles need not abide by the law at all.

For Paul, faith was the key—not the law. And faith, like grace, was a free gift. I wondered if Paul didn't oversimplify things in his belief that the death and resurrection of the Lord were the crux of Jesus' teaching, and hence the Christian faith, and, ultimately, salvation. For the years we knew Jesus were before his death and resurrection, and his focus was different, and his alignment tended more towards living in true discipleship which meant keeping the law as well.

Paul had presented his position already, reiterating what I had said, that God-fearing gentiles need not be converted to Judaism to be saved. Already in Judaism, they can be saved without full conversion.

Then he made the point about the wellbeing of the Christian community. How can we have a true church community centered on Jesus Christ if it is divided—two-tiered—and could not eat and drink and pray together? And so, he emphasized unity in practice. This, of course, would erase the law completely for all Christians, and brought stern disapproval from many. It was a step too far for James, John, and most of the elders.

As far as I knew, Paul taught little of the life and works of the Lord— the miracles, sayings, morality, parables of Jesus. Apparently, he did occasionally reference them, as he must have learned from his adherents, but essentially, he ignored the "heaven on earth" preaching, and looked forward to a day of judgment. He abandoned the Jewish apocalypse for the Christian one. Jesus was no longer the Messiah, the liberator of Israel, but the God of heaven and earth—and savior of humanity.

He was putting Jesus on par with God, and I knew that in the future, this would alienate Jews further and there would be nothing we could do to stop the rift which would, eventually, tear the church apart, perhaps even divest Christianity of its Jewish origins—if not completely, then in part. This could happen before Jesus returned, and what would he find here then? The Commission fulfilled, or failed?

Now I saw the full impact of my conversion of Cornelius, and the command to preach to all nations. But were the Jews right? Preach only to the Jews of all nations, as they said? Also, they said that on the last day, and only then, all nations would come to see the one true God in his glory and power over all peoples. If that was the case, I had erred grievously.

Still, the present had to be dealt with. The mass conversion of gentiles outside Jerusalem and in Judea was a pressing fact. If we denied them salvation outside the law it would condemn the gentiles and negate their conversion. We had to take Jesus at his word that all nations will be given the knowledge of salvation but that the God of Israel must be worshiped, and no other God. The God of Israel was essential for salvation, not the law.

Just before Paul came, James and I decided that, in general, the gentiles would be allowed to adhere outside the law but certain of the laws, such as the Noahide laws, would be maintained. John agreed, and James said he would present the notion to the council, as the meeting was to be called.

The actual meeting with Paul and Barnabas was low-keyed. Paul and Barnabas outlined their success with the Jews, the gentiles, and even the pagans during their missionary time. Paul then detailed his gospel that belief in the death of Jesus for our sins, and the belief in his resurrection, were sufficient for salvation and eternal life. Of course he recognized that love of God and one's neighbor were scripturally obligatory and that faith would enhance these as Christian practices.

It was simply put as always by Paul. He stated his case and asked if we consented or not, and James spoke that consent was given but that all Christians—Jews and gentiles—must adhere to the laws acknowledging the one true God of Israel, and refrain from fornication, eating of blood, meat of strangled or live animals, and idolatry. Circumcision would not be required by gentiles. With that announcement about one in three left the meeting in disgust or anger, turning their backs on us, swirling their cloaks behind them.

Paul, however, was gratified, and James and I accepted the inevitable, but it was without gladness, for we had set the standard, and it was to be a new standard according to Paul's insistence. We knew what we had done, and there was enmity within the meeting, and after. Paul declared himself again apostle to the gentiles and predicted a great inundation of converts, for there was no hindrance now, and the Scriptures would be fulfilled through Jesus Christ.

That was all we could ask. Of course, the zealots demanded more, but for now, certain customs would be maintained. But that was how the meeting unfolded.

25

APOSTLES AND ADVOCATES

AFTER THE MEETING, PAUL WAS anxious to return to his missionary work, and we talked in my home that evening. "I know James, and I know you, Cephas. You were the authority behind the decree. James wanted full enactment of the laws."

"We agreed together," I said.

"You are sad, Cephas."

"Sad? I'm just not sure if it was what Jesus wanted. He said he came to fulfill the law, not to destroy it."

"You must see how he has fulfilled the law with the new covenant. All he did and said culminated in this death and resurrection. That is the reason for everything—including the law—and replacing the law with the saving gift of grace."

"Yes. I know your position. But I fear for the future of the church."

"In what way?"

"It will fall out of our hands—Jewish hands—and turn into what, I don't know."

"Perhaps, but what of it?"

"You cannot see it? If the law is not accepted then how can they accept our Lord God when he is the law?"

"There is no question that the God of Israel is the God of the Christians."

I said that once the law was abolished it was not difficult to abolish tradition and customs which were made and given in praise of our Lord God, by his decree, and for his greater glory. "I fear Israel will be diminished because of the agreement, not enhanced, and with Israel, the God of our fathers. But if we can't agree on such meanings and interpretations here, as his apostles and direct disciples, what does it mean for the future? The division of opinion will be even greater. If we cannot agree on something like eating with gentiles, then future divisions may be tumultuous."

Paul replied that Jesus was the Son of God and the light of the world. What man can say that and be taken seriously? But our Lord said it, and he was demonstrating his Godship with his Father. "There is only ever one God, Cephas, and through Jesus he will be revealed to and accepted by the world and glorified, and so will Judaism—the forebear of a new covenant."

I then asked him how the pagans received his word in Lystra and Iconium. He said the same as everywhere; some were convinced and converted, others planned to kill him. But he said strangely that in Lystra they treated he and Barnabas as gods, like Zeus and Hermes, after they saw some of their miracles.

"What did you do?"

"We revoked them in the harshest terms. One day, Cephas, their temples will be churches. And they will understand that a God has come among them, but not Zeus or Hermes."

"But what do they know of the God of Israel?"

"Nothing. But we say to them three things they must do—abandon their idols and worship the one, true, universal God, and acknowledge that he sent his Son to save us from sin to bring us to eternal life through his death and resurrection. And then the church, as the body of Christ, will take on a life of its own."

I said he spoke well and we hugged and kissed and shook hands, and as he left, he turned to me and said, "Cephas, I will preach to the gentiles, strong and forthright in the Areopagus, and you shall proclaim the gospel from the summit of Mount Sinai."

"Yes, but if you really know me, Paul, then seek me on the Capitoline Hill when you enter Babylon. For I will be there."

APPENDIX I

Map of The Holy Lands in the Time of Jesus

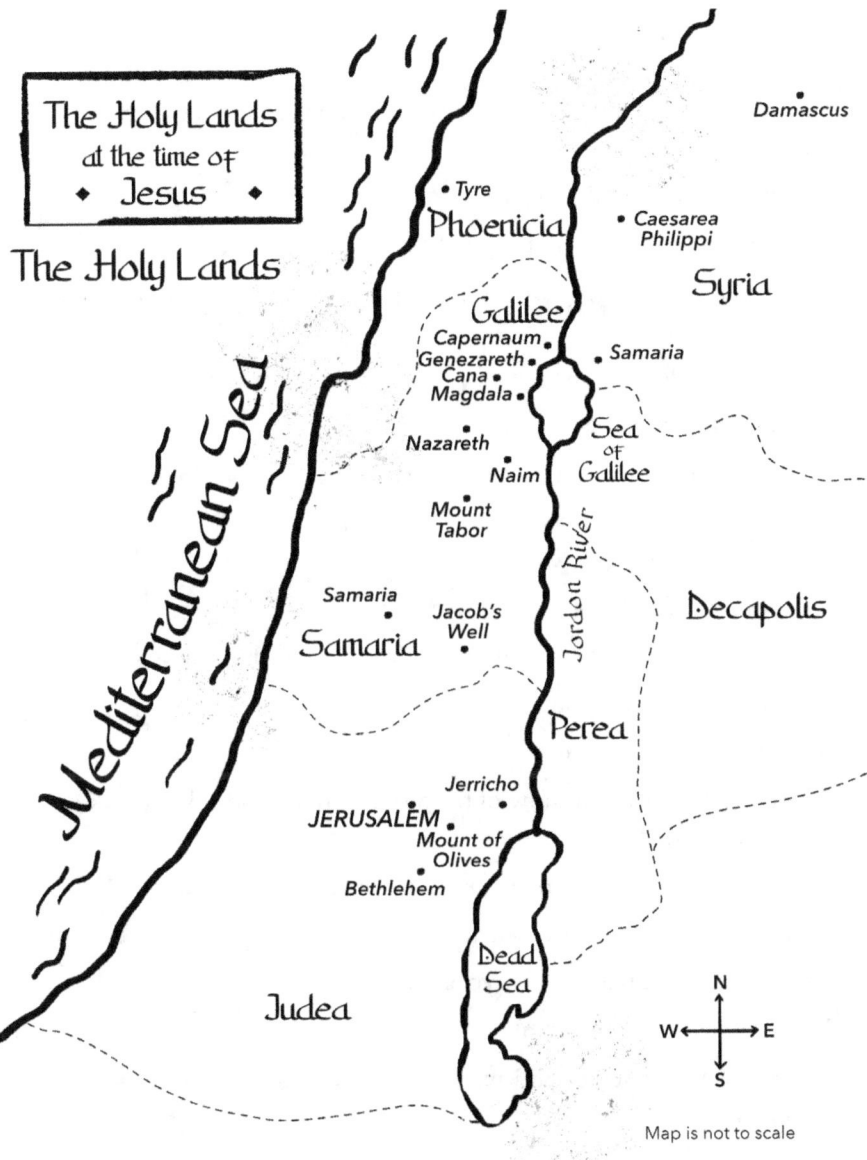

The Holy Lands
at the time of
◆ Jesus ◆

The Holy Lands

Damascus

Tyre

Phoenicia

Caesarea
Philippi

Syria

Galilee

Capernaum
Genezareth
Cana
Magdala

Samaria

Mediterranean Sea

Nazareth

Naim

Sea
of
Galilee

Mount
Tabor

Samaria

Jacob's
Well

Samaria

Jordan River

Decapolis

Perea

Jerricho

JERUSALEM
Mount of
Olives

Bethlehem

Dead
Sea

Judea

N
W — E
S

Map is not to scale

Appendix II
Places Mentioned in the Text

Antioch—In ancient Syria and Pisidia; Antakya, a modern city in Turkey.

Bethany—Near Jerusalem; West Bank.

Bethlehem—Arab city in the West Bank.

Bethsaida—Northern shore of the Sea of Galilee; archaeological site; uninhabited.

Caesarea Philippi—Northern Israel; modern-day nature reserve.

Cana—Arab city in Israel.

Capernaum—Northern shore of Sea of Galilee; archaeological site; uninhabited.

Corinth—Corinth, Greece.

Damascus—Capital of modern-day Syria.

Decapolis—Region spanning parts of modern Jordan, Syria, and Israel.

Ephesus—Selçuk, Turkey.

Galilee—Northern Israel.

Genezareth—Western shore of the Sea of Galilee; today known as Kibbutz Ginosar.

Gerasa—Judea; exact whereabouts unknown.

Gethsemane—Jerusalem, Israel.

Jacob's Well—Samaria, near Sychar; West Bank.

Jericho—Jericho, West Bank.

Judea—West of the Jordan River; today also known as Judea and Samaria.

Machaerus—Jordan; historical site.

Magdala—Western shore of the Sea of Galilee; archaeological site.

Appendix II

Mount of Olives—Jerusalem, Israel.

Mount Sinai—Jabal Musa? Sinai Peninsula, Egypt.

Mount Tabor—Lower Galilee, Israel.

Nazareth—Arab city within Israel.

Perea—East of the Jordan River; in modern Jordan.

Qumran—Northwestern shore of Dead Sea; archaeological site; uninhabited.

Samaria—Near Nablus, West Bank.

Sea of Galilee—Northern Israel.

Tyra and Sidon—Historical cities in Lebanon; have been continually inhabited.

Bibliography

Ahl, Dave. "Jesus's 46 Parables in Chronological Order: Christian Bible Study ~ Introduction and 26 Lessons." Swapmeetdave, September 2025. https://swapmeetdave.com/Bible/Parables/index.htm.

Beecher, Willis J. "Paul's Visits to Jerusalem." The University of Chicago Press: Journals, 1893. https://archive.org/metadata/jstor-3135182.

Bible Ref.com. "What Does Luke 9:53 Mean?" https://www.bibleref.com/Luke/9/Luke-9-53.html.

The Catholic Encyclopedia. "St. Paul." New York: Robert Appleton Company, 1911. https://www.newadvent.org/cathen/11567b.htm.

Cook, Steven R. "The Call of Matthew." Thinking on Scripture (blog), 2021. https://thinkingonscripture.com/2021/01/24/the-call-of-matthew/.

Encyclopedia.com. "Antioch." May 18, 2018. https://www.encyclopedia.com/history/asia-and-africa/ancient-history-middle-east/antioch.

Ehrman, Bart. "On Early Judaism and the Conception of the Afterlife." Literary Hub, April 8, 2020. https://lithub.com/on-early-judaism-and-its-conception-of-the-afterlife/.

Elior, Rachel. "What Jews Believed About the Soul." My Jewish Learning. https://www.myjewishlearning.com/article/jewish-spirituality-and-the-soul/.

Facts and Details. "Saint Peter: His life, Leadership, and Death and Relationship with Jesus." March 2024. https://europe.factsanddetails.com/article/entry-648.html.

Fesko, J. V. "'Works of the Law' in Paul." Westminster Seminary California. https://www.wscal.edu/resource/works-of-the-law-in-paul.

Gardner, Ryan S. "Jesus Christ and the Feast of the Tabernacles." Religious Educator 13.3 (2012) 109–27. https://rsc.byu.edu/vol-13-no-3-2012/jesus-christ-feast-tabernacles.

The Interactive Life of Jesus. "Perean Ministry," December 3, 2008. https://interactivelifeofjesus.com/perean-ministry-introduction.

Joannie6535. "A Blessing & a Curse—Capernaum." Birding Boomers (blog), June 20, 2022. https://birdingboomers.com/2022/06/20/a-blessing-a-curse-capernaum/.

Johnwijngaards.com. "Capernaum." https://www.johnwijngaards.com/publications/galilee/galilee2.shtml.

Kellett, Cy. "When Peter Met Jesus." Catholic Answers (blog), July 2, 2021. https://shop.catholic.com/blog/when-peter-met-jesus.

Kirsch, Johann Peter. "St. Peter, Prince of the Apostles." In The Catholic Encyclopedia 11. New York: Robert Appleton Company, 1911. http://www.newadvent.org/cathen/11744a.htm.

Maas, Anthony J. "Jesus Christ: God the Son, Messiah of Israel." Catholic Answers. https://www.catholic.com/encyclopedia/jesus-christ.

———. "Resurrection of Jesus Christ." In *The Catholic Encyclopedia* 12. New York: Robert Appleton Company, 1911. https://www.newadvent.org/cathen/12789a.htm.

Matthew, P. G. "Paul Preaches to Pagans." Grace Valley Christian Center, December 13, 1998. https://gracevalley.org/sermon/paul-preaches-to-pagans.

Moffic, Evan. "Do Jews Believe in an Afterlife?" Reform Judaism.org, 2025. https://reformjudaism.org/beliefs-practices/lifecycle-rituals/death-mourning/do-jews-believe-afterlife.

Murphy-O'Connor, Jerome. "Peter's Home." Bible Odyssey, June 20, 2017. https://www.bibleodyssey.org/articles/peters-house/.

Never Thirsty: Like the Master Ministries. "Samaritans Reject Jesus." https://www.neverthirsty.org/bible-studies/ministry-in-galilee-late-a-d-32/samaritans-reject-jesus.

OnePage. "Chorazin, Bethsaida, and Capernaum—The Cities That Did Not Repent." https://www.onepagebiblesummary.com/bat/bat_06.php.

Rose, Or N. "Heaven and Hell in Jewish Tradition." My Jewish Learning. https://www.myjewishlearning.com/article/heaven-and-hell-in-jewish-tradition.

Samdahl, Don. "Jesus vs. Paul." Doctrine.org, October 10, 2024. https://doctrine.org/jesus-vs-paul.

Sanders, E. P., et al. "The Context of Jesus' Career." Britannica, August 21, 2025. https://www.britannica.com/biography/Jesus/The-context-of-Jesus-career.

———. "The Jewish Religion in the 1st Century." Britannica, September 17, 2025. https://www.britannica.com/biography/Jesus/The-Jewish-religion-in-the-1st-century.

———. "Relation of Jesus's Teaching to the Jewish Law." Britannica, August 21, 2025. https://www.britannica.com/biography/Jesus/The-relation-of-Jesus-teaching-to-the-Jewish-law.

Schachterle, Josha. "Saint Peter: Quest for the Historical Apostle Peter." Bart Ehrman, September 21, 2023. https://www.bartehrman.com/saint-peter/.

Smith, Patrick Scott. "The Journeys of Paul the Apostle." World History Encyclopedia, August 15, 2024. https://www.worldhistory.org/article/2515/the-journeys-of-paul-the-apostle/.

Stewart, Jameson. "5 Accusations Jesus Brought Against the Scribes and Pharisees." Centred on Christ (blog), April 19, 2022. https://centeredonchrist.substack.com/p/5-accusations-jesus-brought-against.

Strange, John. "Who is the Greatest?" Bible Study Headquarters, 2024. https://www.biblestudyheadquarters.com/blog/who-is-the-greatest.

Studies of Religion II. "Paul of Tarsus." https://lumensor.weebly.com/paul-of-tarsus.html.

Totally History. "Simon Peter." 2020. https://totallyhistory.com/biblical-history/simon-peter-the-apostle.

Wayne, Luke. "What Was the Subject of John the Baptist's Teaching?" CARM, February 23, 2016. https://carm.org/other-questions/what-was-the-subject-of-john-the-baptists-preaching.

Wikipedia. "Atonement in Judaism." December 27, 2024. https://en.wikipedia.org/wiki/Atonement_in_Judaism.

———. "Capernaum." June 9, 2025. https://en.wikipedia.org/wiki/Capernaum.

———. "Commissioning of the Twelve Apostles." May 21, 2025. https://en.wikipedia.org/wiki/Commissioning_of_the_Twelve_Apostles.

Bibliography

———. "Incident at Antioch." July 3, 2025. https://en.wikipedia.org/wiki/Incident_at_Antioch.

———. "Jesus's Interaction with Women." May 24, 2025. https://en.wikipedia.org/wiki/Jesus%27s_interactions_with_women.

———. "Jewish Eschatology." August 12, 2025. https://en.wikipedia.org/wiki/Jewish_eschatology.

———. "Parable of the Unjust Judge." August 30, 2025. https://en.wikipedia.org/wiki/Parable_of_the_Unjust_Judge.

———. "Philip the Apostle." September 1, 2025. https://en.wikipedia.org/wiki/Philip_the_Apostle.

———. "Samaritan Woman at the Well." September 1, 2025. https://en.wikipedia.org/wiki/Samaritan_woman_at_the_well.

———. "Woes to the Unrepentant Cities." August 27, 2025. https://en.wikipedia.org/wiki/Woes_to_the_unrepentant_cities.

www.ingramcontent.com/pod-product-compliance
Lightning Source LLC
Chambersburg PA
CBHW051131260626
47170CB00005B/1770